Dedication:

This book is dedicated to my fairy-tale husband, John who is my inspiration and muse. He's my ideas man. He is the love of my life. It took me 34 years to find him and I never want to be without him again. He's the other half of my soul. Thank you baby for everything!

This book is a work of fiction. Any references to historical events or real people are used fictitiously. Other names, characters, places and incidents are the product of the author's imagination, and any resemblance to actual events or persons, living or dead, is entirely coincidental.

Vampirical Lyrical Publishing Co.

Cleveland, Ohio

Table of Contents:

Chapter One: My Emergence

"It was in the 1400's in Romania that I was born again. I had been the King's Constable, keeper of his horses and protector of his people, defender of mankind. I had been sitting in my office one night after a saloon brawl, guarding the prisoners when in walked a mystery man. He floated in the door, staying in the shadows, darkness always covering his face holding a curious outline. He had been dressed in a long black cape with a top hat and cane, something only reserved for the older wealthy class. He walked right up to me and spoke in a deeply quiet whisper I could barely hear, shadow still covering his face.

"Skender, I can change your life for you, give you one that never ends and allows you to reinvent yourself over and over, but you have a choice. You can choose to sit where you are, a peasant watching over the King's property or a King with others watching over your property" came the seductively smooth voice in my ear.

'Who wouldn't perk up at the thought of being his own King?' I thought to myself. I was young, had large unobtainable dreams and sitting behind that desk none of them would come true. I stood up and nodded my head at him slowly. The man lunged for me, grabbed me around the neck and waist and suddenly I felt a large pain in the side of my neck. He drank from me, so deeply that it weakened me and I fell to the floor yet he still stayed attached to my neck. He continued to drink until I passed out but not before seeing the eyes of the men peering out from between the bars, staring at me in horror. When I awoke, I was in my own bed in my small two room hut on the King's land. I sat up in bed sweating and with a start and when I felt the pain in my neck, I reached up to it and found it bandaged by an unknown hand. I had little memory of the previous night's events though I remembered the shadowy figure and a dream I'd had as if I'd slept the whole night. I dreamt of a crimson haired maiden, one with alabaster skin, warm hands and a delicate heart. Her image was so clear that I could not get her out of my mind yet she wasn't anyone I'd ever seen before or knew now. I stepped outside into the noon day sun and my skin started to tingle and eventually burn. The light was so bright that it blinded my eyes and a searing pain shot through my head. I ran back into my house, quickly closing the door behind me and leaned against it while adjusting back to the cool darkness of my hut. I instantly felt better in the dark and there learned my first lesson of my 'new' being. The shadowed man had left me so I had to learn the limits and abilities of my new existence on my own. I continued to patrol the lands from sun down to sun up and hired another man to fill in for me during the daytime. I started feeding on the transients that passed through town which were luckily plentiful. I had learned that I needed to drink blood, just like that man had done to me that night, to survive. It had been awful at first but I'd learned I'd turn into a ravenous beast if I didn't so it didn't take me long to learn that's what I needed. My new abilities quickly became evident when I attempted to restrain some criminals and overpowered them easily. So, as you can see, while I tried to keep the peace, I was learning to keep the peace and avoid the beast within myself as well. I enjoyed helping others and couldn't just sit around and wallow in my new existence. Another of the benefits was my 'animal' magnetism I had on the young women of the village. I quickly made my way through them again and again, searching for the woman from my dreams, but they never turned against me. No one knew my extra-curricular activities at night. Each century I moved around the world, worked as a Constable or law enforcement agent until the 1700's when I had tragedy befall me.

I had fallen in love with a beautiful socialite who worshipped the ground I walked on. She was not the woman from my dream but I had long given up hope of ever finding her. There was a break in at her house one night while I was out hunting and she was killed.

There had been nothing I could have done about it either as a boyfriend, law man or vampire. I'd lost my trust in mankind and decided to abandon them, except for sustenance purposes. I became a recluse until I heard of the Regime. There were tales about them across the lands of the existence of other vampires and vampire hunters alike. Those tales spoke of freedom finding one's self, relief from the mundane existence my life had become and belonging somewhere. I traveled far and wide looking for this Regime until one day, my Maker met me in a dark alley. He led me to the outskirts of the 'promised land' and then proposed a new bride for me for eternity. When I declined, he hissed, turned to smoke and disappeared into the night. I made my way into the complex after being stripped of my belongings, searched, questioned, tested and then taken in as a brother. I was trained in the ways of the vampire. I was trained to become an assassin for the Regime for they often had rogue vampires that would turn up that needed hunting and finally extermination. I served for the Regime for fifty years before I decided they hadn't fulfilled any of their promises of a new life or belonging.

I traveled the continent looking for excitement but after living a life on the constant hunt, nothing interested me. I again became a recluse until the 1980's when crazy music invoked something within me and made me want to emerge and take note of the new times. I'd always been a fan of music but this music aroused the passion in me I'd lost when I lost my Isabella. Such bands as Skid Row, Bon Jovi, Metallica, Kiss, Twisted Sister, Slayer, Ozzy Osbourne, Motorhead, Guns N' Roses, Iron Maiden, Dokken, Scorpions, Sepultura and Black Sabbath woke the demon in me and brought me back to life. This is my new life.

Chapter Two: The Police Academy

"MR. SKENDER! ARE YOU PAYING ATTENTION?" boomed the Sargent in the academy class. I sat there, looking out the window at the foggy evening darkness, wishing I was out hunting in it when the Sargent caught me and singled me out.

"Yes Sargent Fischer. I'm paying attention, sorry Sir" I back peddled. I had been going to the night police academy to become a trained police officer so I could defend mankind again. This music that had awakened me made me want to attend these spectacles they called concerts and I needed currency to do so, thus pushing me towards a career for the next couple decades and I wanted to see how the lawman profession had changed since I'd been away. Tonight, after class, was going to be the first time we met up with real Policemen and rode along with them in their cars for a few hours. I'd been looking forward to this day since my awakening. Though 500 years had passed since my creation, I didn't look a day over twenty-three years old so I looked wet behind the ears though I'd worked circles around my fellow recruits over the centuries.

"Then let me repeat. What is a 10-54, a 502 and a code purple?"

"A 10-54 is a possible dead body, a 502 is drunk driving and a code purple is gang activity" I replied.

"Um, okay. Next time please look like you are paying attention" the Sargent said and moved on around the class asking questions and continuing to put people on the spot.

Eventually class time was over and we went outside and stood next to our assigned officers at the cars. The Patrolmen shook hands with the classmen and we got into the vehicle for the ride. They rode their designated area for the allotted timeframe in almost absolute silence. The Patrolman assigned to Skendar occasionally questioned him but he knew his stuff forwards and backwards. They came across a code purple twice that night and had to call in backup to break up some fights. Otherwise, the night was quiet. From then on, after class, each student was assigned one week with a different Patrolman to ride the city streets of Cleveland, Ohio. Skender felt like he was in his glory. He loved being back out on the streets protecting the people and doing his duty. He would feed each night before he came into class/work and might feed again afterwards if he was really exhausted. The one evening, there was a suspicious call that he and his partner took. One that hit too close to home.

Chapter Three: My First Case

When they arrived on scene, the two men walked up the alley, pushing through the crowd of people towards the body laying on the ground under the sheet. When they arrived, they lifted the sheet and immediately Skender could smell it. It was no human who had committed this crime and though it had stumped the other officers, he knew the type of 'person' who did it, now he just had to find out which one. He had come to know so many of them over the centuries but this one left no 'calling card'. The body was already blue and in decomposition because it had been drained of blood and there were two teeth marks on the left side of the corpse's neck. '*A Vampire*' he thought to himself. A vampire had killed this poor soul, drained his blood and dumped his body carelessly in this alley to die. He was going to have to call in the Regime to find out who did it and take care of him for 'human' methods would not kill this vampire as he was strong. That was obvious to Skender by looking at the bite site.

Chapter Four: The Detective's Take Over

A cell phone rang somewhere in the dark distance. A thin feminine hand reached out from under a pile of covers and quickly dragged it back underneath.

"Hello?" a soft voice mumbled from under the covers.

"Fleece!" came the shout from the other end of the phone. She instantly sat upright in bed at full attention. "Alexis? Are you there?" came the gruff voice again.

"Yes Sir. I'm here" she said awake now.

"Fleece, we have an 11-44 (dead body) so you better get your butt down here" he demanded.

"Yes Sir. I'm on my way Sir" she said as he hung up in a hurry. She flipped the covers off and looked at the clock. 3 AM. It was going to be a long day.

Forty-five minutes later when she arrived at the scene, she was still groggy and mumbled, "Badge number 38135, 10-86" (meaning she'd arrived on the scene) into the vehicle's radio before exiting the car. As she was walking towards the crowd of people her Lieutenant came bounding towards her.

"Geez! What took you so long? Did you have to iron your skirt?" he demeaning sneered.

"No, I do all my ironing the night before" she snapped back and then hung her head when she saw the look of death she got from him.

"Let's go Fleece. It's already been too long waiting for you. I'm sure every local Cleveland Cop has trounced through the crime scene by now" he huffed. She followed him down the alley behind the businesses at Lorain Ave and W. 131st street. Usually a quiet alley, today held a dead guy with a bleeding head and a 4X4 sitting next to him with blood on it. *'This is too easy'* Alexis thought to herself. *'The killer didn't bother to clean up, dump the weapon but knew that fingerprints cannot be removed from wood? It was too easy'* she thought again to herself. She tucked in the back of her skirt and knelt down next to the victim. She searched him for identification or receipts but found nothing.

"I already had the guys do that" the Lieutenant said impatiently.

"I like to go over everything myself" she smiled back at him sweetly and went back to searching the body. Just as she pulled back the collar of the dead guy she found what she was looking for. She stood up, brushed off her skirt and walked, in heels, over to her Lieutenant. "It's our vampire. He's back" she said as a look of shock crossed his face.

"How do you know? Did you work the original cases?" the Lieutenant asked. Since he had only been assigned to her precinct a year ago he was only vaguely familiar with the cases.

"Yes. I was the lead Detective on the case for three years. Girls kept turning up a month at a time, with the same marks and exsanguated the same way as our dead guy here" she looked back up the alley at him just lying there, hoping she was dealing with only a copycat for the original killer had been vicious and uncatchable.

"So what happened to the case? I take it you didn't get the guy?" he teased.

"Nope. Case went cold and I was pulled off to do other, more important things" she informed him.

"Well, looks like you're back on the case and I'm assigning you lead but you run everything through me" he said condescendingly. "And this time, get that SOB" he chuckled and walked away. She really did not like that man but since he was her Lieutenant she had to kiss his butt to some extent.

The Coroner showed up and he was leaning over the body when Alexis walked up behind him.

"Miss Fleece!" he said cheerily. "What a wonderful morning, eh?" he asked, looking up at her for an answer.

"Yep. Just great!" she said sourly. The Coroner went back to examining the bloodied head. As he pulled the hair back, he noticed the bite marks and jumped back in alarm.

"Um, Detective?" he said unsure of himself. Alexis just nodded and he nodded back. He knew what the marks meant and how much hard work they were going to have ahead of them. He hoped the killer did not start the same spree and kill so many more people again. He was tired of all those girls in his morgue. He'd never seen anything like it and wasn't prepared for it by any means at the time.

"Thanks Leonard, I mean, Dr. Snow. Please forward me the report as soon as possible. I'm heading back to the house to dig out some old case files."

****

"Mornin' Fleece" came the voice that refocused her eyes on the page of the file she'd been pouring over and brought her back to reality.

"Hey Marty. Where were you this morning?" Alexis asked a little suspicious.

"Had some family business and couldn't leave the kids" he said sheepishly.

"It was no big deal. We just had a dead guy in the alley. But here's the funny thing…he had our old friends' bite marks on him" Alexis said looking for a response from Marty.

"Oh geez! Not again! Are you sure?" he asked, his face turning red with anger and hatred.

"Yep. Hopefully it's a copycat, if not, he's back and he's reconstructing his death list to include men this time" she said.

"Yes, that is odd. So, whatcha' doin' with all those files on your desk?" Marty asked.

"Trying to find a connection between the vics" she announced.

"Didn't we already go through all that at the time of the cases?" Marty asked perplexed.

"Yes but it never hurts to go over them again now that the killer is back and we have to find him this time" Alexis said sternly.

"Yes we do or the new Lieutenant's gonna be all over our butts and I really don't want that. Here" he said reaching towards her. "Give me half the stack and we'll both go over them. Get them done quicker and two sets of eyes are better than one" he smiled at her. She smiled back, handed him some files and went back to pouring over the open file in front of her with a sigh.

Chapter Five: The "Copycat"

Vampire. A deliciously evil smile spread across her face as she fondly remembered her first days as a vampire. Everything was new and through her new vampire eyes she saw things as an infant would. She loved being a vampire for, according to her, the world was hers. She fed on whomever she wished or had a taste for each evening. Her senses were heightened and things always seemed to be in fast forward for her when she moved. She could fly overnight to anywhere in the world and start a new life, completely reinventing herself over the centuries. However, it was always Cleveland that seemed to catch her eye this decade and draw her back.

As she sat on the rooftop watching her wonderfully created scene and swarm of police cars below, she became elated when the infamous Detective Alexis Fleece, badge # 38135 arrived. She had done this just for her. Just to get close to her again as it had been too long. Her hiatus in Italy and Spain was wonderful but she missed her Detective Fleece. They had such a history together. One Alexis wasn't even aware of yet. But she'd figure it out, Lavina was sure of that.

"It was I that laid all those people at your feet" Lavina said out loud, back in her lair. "The wrong-doers. The criminals that escaped punishment due to your lack of ability to perform your job duties without going all commando on people. You lose your temper too easily and that's why we are playing this game of cat and mouse. Oh, how I love games!" Lavina said as she drank her blood from a golden, Sapphire, Emerald, Amethyst and Opal decorated chalice. She liked her blood cold and since she took it from that man a few hours ago it was just to her liking. "He was so gross and disgusting that I hated to even touch him but he was next on our list, Detective" she said between sips. She was sitting on her plush purple velvet throne chair next to the fireplace. She was afraid of fire but it warmed her painfully cold skin. Her familiar, Daniel was more than happy to start her fire for her each night while she was out in search of her next victim. He was a good human, as far as humans go. He always had her blood ready and helped her with anything and everything. He did daytime things she was unable to do herself and yet he managed to be right there at her beckon call when she rose each night. His ambition was to become a vampire someday but for now he was content in his "apprenticeship".

"How easy it was to take over someone else's' work, make them think it is him again, but add in my own addenda. It's time to step things up a bit" Lavina said to herself. "One more victim and then we are heading closer to home."

Chapter Six: The Second Victim

She was sitting at her desk pouring over the recent victim's file again. Slim was her computer geek and he was feeding her more and more information by the moment. The vic' had not been nice guy. He brutally raped and killed a random woman he had picked up out of the downtown streets in broad daylight. He held her captive for three days while raping her repeatedly. The police were closing in on him and he took his hostage and managed to maneuver his way into the middle of Euclid Ave. He then shot the woman in the head while her family looked on from the crowd. He tossed his gun and let the police arrest him. She had been the lead Detective on the case and disobeyed a direct order to "stand down" while cuffing him. Once he had been cuffed she took to berating him and kicking him. Her fellow police officers looked on but didn't interfere until she really got out of control. When the man got his day in court, the case was dismissed with an apology from the police department to the man. The Judge decided he didn't deserve the beating he got and that equaled the time he served already as punishment enough. Alexis always had a hard time with this case. It was her fault he went free and the family of the victim never got any satisfaction or closure. She had been busted down to desk duty for a month until the Chief couldn't take her being in the house, pacing and such so he put her back on the street. She repeatedly beat herself up over this case but this was not the only one like it. She had lost her temper or done things to other offenders that their cases in the past were dismissed as well. This however, was the first case in her long list. The Chief got tired of punishing her so he set her up with a partner in hopes he would be able to reign her in somewhat. She hated working with others. She was a solo Detective and resented the Chief's decision but at least she didn't get some rookie, she got a decorated Detective who'd been on the job for almost 20 years. This, she was thankful for as she didn't have to also be her partners' babysitter.

"Fleece, here" her partner Marty Rodriguez was standing above her handing her a Starbucks Peppermint Mocha, soy, no whipped, just the way she liked it.

"What? How'd you know how I...?" she asked.

"I pay attention. It's part of my job, you know" he said smiling as he sat down at his desk across from hers.

"Thanks" she mumbled, took a delicious sip and went back to pouring over her file.

"Still working on the case I see. Did you get any sleep last night? You look like crap" he said with his eyes showing laughter and leaning forward in his chair.

"No, as a matter of fact I didn't so don't bug me today Rodriguez" Alexis said. Marty crept back to his side of the desk. He leaned back in his chair and put his feet up on the desk, all the while watching her as she huffed and puffed and played with her hair while paging through the file. She suddenly slammed the file shut and leaned back in her chair with her arms folded across her chest.

"There's nothing here" Alexis said perturbed.

"I told you. The case went cold, remember?" Marty said mockingly.

"I just thought if I looked through the pages again, this time I might see something I missed" she trailed off.

"But there's still nothing" he concluded.

"All our resources say it was a vigilante vampire but vampires don't really exist" she said with questioning eyes. As a child she'd believed in vampires but once she grew up and saw the things she'd seen as a street cop, she couldn't believe in vampires anymore. It wasn't rational and all her training in the academy taught her if it didn't seem rational then it wasn't. Just as she was starting to doubt herself a call came in over her walkie.

"Alert Fire and Rescue we have a code 20, acute trauma case. It's a 10-45B, patient is in serious condition. All units are required at Lakewood Park at the corner of Clifton and Belle Avenue in the City of Lakewood to assist" came the male voice in a rush over the walkie. Alexis and Marty looked at each other, grabbed their jackets and ran to the undercover car.

While the City of Lakewood had their own local police department, when a call came in that involved a Cleveland case, Cleveland Detectives were allowed on the scene to investigate. When they arrived on the scene, the ambulance and fire was present and a woman was being wheeled into the ambulance. She had IV tubes and oxygen tubes hanging out of her and she was strapped down to the gurney already.

"Please" Alexis said trying to push the medics aside. "I need to speak with this woman" she said urgently.

"Not tonight. This woman is lucky to be alive. She is the latest victim of 'the vampire' and we have to get her a blood transfusion or she'll die" he said attempting to move Alexis. She didn't move.

"All the more reason I'm coming with you" she said. She motioned for Rodriguez to follow and jumped into the back of the bus as they quickly closed the doors and sped off to Metro Hospital Trauma Unit as the local hospital was too small to deal with such a trauma. Alexis was fine with that for it gave her time to speak with the victim.

"I'm Agent Fleece with the Cleveland Police Department" she said slowly, looking for any sign of recognition from the woman. She nodded 'yes' slowly so Alexis continued. "You are in the back of an ambulance because you were attacked. Did you see your attacker?" she asked trying to sound kind but urgent at the same time. A sudden look of surprise came over the woman and she tried to struggle free from her restraints. She tried to move away from Alexis.

"What's going on over here?" the medic said leaning around Alexis to look at his patient.

"I dunno. Suddenly she became scared and combative when I was just speaking with her" Alexis explained.

"Combative? She's the one that's restrained. I've read about you in the papers. My patient is critical and you are no longer allowed to speak with her and upset her" the medic said pushing Alexis by her leg further down the bench seat so she was away from the head of the victim. "It's alright now ma'am. Let's just get you to the hospital and you'll be ok" he said giving Alexis a sideways glance and then went back to his paperwork.

When they arrived at the hospital, an OR was waiting and Alexis was not permitted to follow the patient whom she had intended not to let out of her sight inside. '*Why had she reacted so violently to me?*' she wondered to herself. A few minutes later, Rodriguez came rushing in but Alexis shook her head 'no' and he looked disappointed.

"Now what?" he said standing against the wall next to her.

"Now we wait. She had a significant reaction to me in the ambulance and I need to know why. We'll find out when she comes out of the transfusion" Alexis explained. She slid down the wall and sat down on the floor to wait outside the OR doors. A couple hours later the doors opened and a very disgruntled doctor came out shaking his head. "How is she doc? When can we get in to see her?" she begged, jumping up off the floor.

"I'm afraid you can't" he said still shaking his head.

"Why?" Rodriguez asked.

"She died on the table. We transfused her blood twice but her heart just finally gave out. It had been so completely drained and then so rushed with blood that her body was unable to keep up with it" he explained. Alexis sunk back down to the floor. This had been the closest they had come to as an eye witness of the killer and now she's become his next victim. Alexis couldn't believe it was happening again. She tried over and over in her head to convince herself it wasn't true but when she looked into her partners' eyes a flood of anger rushed over her.

"Let's go back to the house and see what we can dig up on the vic" Rodriguez said trying to console her.

"I'm up for just about anything right about now" Alexis said and they headed back to the station.

Chapter Seven: Coming For Her

"How sweet it was to have a tainted woman for a change" she said aloud to her empty lair.

She had wanted this one to be special as it would be the last seemingly 'random' victim before it became personal for Detective Fleece. This was the last unknown 'victim' that went to trial and she was sure Detective Fleece would be able to piece the cases together by now.

But the victim…the victim had been a fighter this time. Also, had it not been for the jogger that came by and spooked her, she would have been able to finish the job and not hope for the best. She'd weakened her heart enough that it would give out, which it ended up doing, luckily for her. The next time was planned perfectly and luck was not going to be a part of the equation. There was going to be no mistaking the fact that 'the vampire' has made this war personal. If Fleece hasn't already figured it out by then, this will push her over the edge.

"I want her to know that I'm coming for her, slowly making my way back to her. She's a smart cookie and will figure it out soon."

Chapter Eight: The Pieces Start To Come Together

Again, she was sitting at her desk, pouring over last nights' events when Rodriguez came in and sat down at his desk. He was amazed at Fleeces' work ethic but he'd seen her type before. Young, ambitious cop that made Detective by twenty-three, trying to prove to the boys that she's just as good as they are even though she's a woman. Yeah, he's seen it but she can actually back it up except for her pride and tomboyish toughness came through too often. That's why the Chief asked him to keep an eye on her. He hated babysitting but he was close to retirement and figured he could get worse duties so he agreed.

"Find out anything new on our Jane Doe?" he asked as he leaned back in his chair and put his feet up on the desk like he always did.

"Actually, I did and she just happens to be Margaret Swenson" Alexis said proudly.

"THE Margaret Swenson?" he asked bewildered, dropping his feet from the desk and leaning forward. Alexis nodded 'yes'. "How'd you find that out?"

"Coroner ran her prints and since she was previously in the system they came back as a hit. Are you familiar with the case?" she asked.

"Of course I am. It was the school teacher that was molesting young boys. You set up a sting operation and posed as a young boy in a chat room and when you met you took her into custody. Judge thought it was entrapment and threw the case out" he recited proudly, still recalling many of the terrified faces of the boys that took the stand against her and her actions.

"Yes, well, I got blamed for that one going awry and was put on probation again for inappropriate behavior" Alexis pouted.

"I never agreed with that decision" Rodriguez said in support.

"Here's what I've gathered though. These two murders were somehow connected to me but I don't yet know how or why. Who do I know who could be doing this and why are they doing it? To hurt me? I don't understand" Alexis said perplexed.

"Why you? I'm sure you have tons of enemies but why would this 'vampire' thing target you?" Marty asked.

"I'm not sure but I intend to find out" Alexis said determined. She sat silently in her chair, obviously deep in thought. Marty watched her cautiously. She was so far into her own world that she jumped off her chair when her phone rang.

"Fleece!" came the usual shout from the Lieutenant. "We got a double 187 (homicide) at 11722 Longmead near Puritas in Cleveland. Get Marty and get both your asses over there now" he demanded.

■■

As she stood over the two sheeted bodies, Alexis' phone blared in her pocket. She pulled it out and it was her mom. She hesitated but answered it anyway hoping to brush her off quickly.

"My poor Rosita!" she exclaimed into the phone.

"What? Mom? What are you talking about?" Alexis said irritated.

"Rosita's twins were killed last night and now that the police are investigating and she's been discovered as an illegal. She is going to be deported back to Bahia, Brazil where her family lives. I'm going to be out of a housekeeper. Do something!" she insisted. Alexis' head started spinning. 'Twins...killed last night?' She immediately snapped the phone shut and bent over to lift the sheets on the dead bodies. Sure enough they were two twin boys of Brazilian descent. She replaced the sheet and went off to find Rosita. She tracked her down in the kitchen, sitting at the table with a cup of coffee.

"Rosita" Alexis said entering the kitchen. Rosita rose, ran to her and hugged her crying into her shoulder.

"Mi filihas" (my sons) she sobbed. "Por que?" she asked.

"Rosita. Tell me what happened" Alexis prodded. The woman told a story of a leather clad creature that was waiting in the house for them when she came home from the grocery store with her boys. The creature tied her up and made her watch as she mutilated her sons and left the dreaded fang marks on their necks. A neighbor heard her screams and called 911. As the sirens came the creature disappeared off into the night, leaving her tied up and her two twin boys dead on the floor in front of her. Alexis hugged her and left her in the kitchen to find her partner. She recounted the incredible story to Marty whose eyes grew wider and wider as she retold the story.

"So, no details on this 'creature', huh?" he asked.

"Unfortunately, no. She was a hysterical Brazilian woman and I didn't want to push her more tonight. I'll contact her in the next day or two and try to get more details. She's also got to deal with deportation as she's here illegally so she's not in a good place right now" Alexis explained. Marty nodded.

When they returned to her desk, her phone's red light was flashing indicating she had a voicemail. As she checked it, she sighed in frustration at her mothers' persistence.

"You're a police woman. Can't you do something for Rosita? I can't lose my housekeeper!" she demanded."Also, your Aunt Bea called and your grandmother passed away in the nursing home. Visiting hours will be tomorrow and the funeral will be on Friday." Alexis hung up deflated and emotional. She instantly put her head in her hands on her desk and sobbed lightly. She felt a cold hand on her shoulder and looked up. Marty was standing there looking down at her with soft eyes.

"What's going on Alexis? This isn't like you" he asked kindly. Alexis just shook her head 'no' with tears streaming down her face.

"I can't believe she's gone" Alexis sobbed. Marty pulled her into his embrace. "She had stage 4 cancer so it wasn't like we weren't expecting it but I still didn't expect it today" she said. "It's been such a crappy day." Marty hugged her tighter. She noticed how cold his body felt against hers. His touch was as cold as ice and his cold breath sent a tingle down her spine. She pulled away and looked deep into his eyes. *Could it be? Could he be?* she wondered. He did disappear at night and didn't show up to evening calls sighting 'family' obligations but could they be real? Does he even have a family? She would have to investigate and find out. She knew very little about this man, her partner but intended to find out as much as possible. She made a mental note to contact Slim at her first free moment.

■ ■

Slim ran Rodriguez through the system as the persistence of Alexis whom he knew would not give him a break until he did. Report after report came back where Marty was missing or unavailable on night calls or for evening duty. Alexis was slowly starting to wrap her head around the facts. 'Missing nights, unavailable, cold skin, could he be a vampire but how did he walk during the day?' she wondered. Just then Marty came in and Slim minimized his screen and Alexis snapped out of her trance.

"Whatcha' guys doin'?" he asked.

"Nothing" the two answered in unison. Marty gave them a suspicious look and then headed to his desk. Alexis thanked Slim and headed to hers.

"Marty?" Alexis started.

"Yes?" he answered.

"Where have you been the last couple nights that you couldn't come on calls with me?" she asked point blank. He stammered before answering:

"I've been out at the bar a lot. It's not been going so good with the Mrs., so I've been out getting hammered each night. Didn't want to report for duty drunk" he attempted to explain. Alexis nodded in acceptance but deep down she knew something wasn't right.

"Well" he said changing the subject, "I still have paperwork to do on the double 187 of the Brazilian twins" he said and got up from his desk to go get the paperwork forms. Alexis was left sitting there alone to ponder his truth and lies, but why the lies. '*What was he covering up?*' she wondered.

Chapter Nine: The Connection Becomes Clear

Another unwelcomed call in the middle of the night sent Alexis into a tizzy. This time it was Dr. Snow.

"Alexis. Did I wake you?" he asked when she answered groggily.

"No. It's fine. What's up?" she asked.

"Well, I'm doing an autopsy on your grandmother at your mothers' request and I found something you should know about" he explained.

"What is it?" she asked trying to decide what was so important that he needed to call her in the middle of the night about a dead woman.

"It's just that…well…your grandmother has our friends' bite marks on her wrist" he finally got it out after stammering and trying to beat around the bush.

"She what!" Alexis demanded practically jumping upright in bed.

"Alexis. I'm sorry but I thought you'd like to know before I have to turn the report over to the police" he said. Alexis took everything in her to push down her anger to say calmly:

"You're right Dr. Snow. Thank you for letting me know. I'll see you in the morning". They hung up. Alexis laid there trying to go back to sleep but couldn't. She tried to think of all the reasons the vampire would do this to her grandmother and nothing about it seemed random. As she lay there and thought about all the cases and her grandmother she realized the connection:

"Me" she said aloud. "The vampire's after me."

Somewhere far away in her lair, Lavina was chuckling to herself. She could see Alexis in her crystal ball just laying there in bed and come to her conclusion. '*The simple look of horror on her face was priceless*' she thought to herself. Now, maybe, she will connect the dots back to me. Lavina hoped for the best as Detective Fleece was getting closer and closer. It would end in a duel of the greatest proportions but also the greatest of the centuries for Lavina.

Chapter Ten: The Common Link

The following morning, Alexis was running late after not being able to sleep most of the night. She had on her usual skirt and heels but looked somehow disheveled. As she walked in the door to the house she dropped a file and bent over to pick it up. Rodriguez rushed to her side to help her.

"Boy, you look rough this morning" he observed.

"It's no wonder you're going through marital problems with an attitude like that" Alexis shot back as she scooped up the file and headed to her desk. She started a suspect board with all the suspects that have died in the past few days with the bite marks. She put herself at the top and everyone else below her.

"I don't understand. You're the common link?" Rodriguez said in dismay.

"That's right. It came to me last night. Someone or something is targeting me but why is the question".

"That's going to be a hard one. We all know you've made a lot of enemies over the past five years as Detective" he said.

"I know and thanks for the reminder" she grimaced.

"Where do we start?" he asked.

"Well…my only guess is…I have no idea. I don't know what this creature is, all I know is that it's not a scorned relative so it's got to be something inhuman."

"So you're saying this thing is supernatural?" he guffawed.

"Yes. In a way. I suggest we consult the local voodoo priestess and see what she comes up with" Alexis said.

"I can't believe you believe in that crap" Rodriguez said disgusted.

"It's the only thing I think we have to go on" she said grabbing her jacket and heading towards the door. "You coming?"

"I guess but nothing about me this time, got it?" he said stubbornly.

"Sure thing."

They headed down into the slums of East Cleveland, Hough Ave to be exact. That's where Alexis knew she would find the voodoo woman sitting on her porch. This voodoo woman had helped Alexis solve many cases and she trusted her immensely. She was always on point and knew her craft well. As they pulled up to the house, she was sitting on her porch fanning herself just as Alexis had predicted. Alexis and Rodriguez walked up to her and bowed and Alexis stepped forward.

"I am in need of some guidance. Could you help me Mother?" Alexis asked.

"But of course child. I knew you'd be coming to me soon and here you are. Let's go to my basement where it's cooler so we can talk" she suggested. The three of them entered a house that was as hot as an oven and loaded with people. They made their way through the people and down to the basement. The old woman sat in a chair on a rug with a table in front of her and to the side of her that had potions and herbs on it. She motioned for Alexis and Rodriguez to sit in front of her. Alexis sat but Rodriguez stood back against the wall.

"He does not believe" she said more than asked. Alexis nodded 'yes'. "Tisk, Tisk" the woman said, shook her head but proceeded to organize things for Alexis. She took a handful of old bones out of a purple velvet bag, tossed them into a wooded bowl that smoked when they made contact with the bowl. She blew the smoke away and stared intently into the bowl. Alexis couldn't help but lean forward for a look into the bowl knowing damn well she wouldn't know what she was looking at anyway. The woman stared and stared in the bowl with a disgruntled face. Finally she sat the bowl down and looked up at Alexis.

"You are having a hard time at work, yes?" she asked. Alexis nodded 'yes'. "Something supernatural or not of this century is after you" she remarked sadly. "Beware of this being for it could be your undoing. Also, you will need to make amends with your mother soon, do not hesitate. Here" she said, rummaging through the stones on the table to her right. She handed Alexis a Rose Quartz and an Obsidian stone. "These will protect you. The light one absorbs and emits good energy and the black one absorbs negative energy so your body doesn't have to do it. Keep them on you at all times. Be on your way now" she said, shooing them upstairs. Rodriguez was the first upstairs as all this 'mumbo jumbo' scared him. Alexis just giggled at him, put the stones in her jacket pocket and thanked the old lady with a deep bow.

On the way back to the house, Rodriguez questioned Alexis.

"So, you're mother huh? I've never heard you talk about her. I just assumed she was deceased" he said trying to sound gentle.

"Well, we all know what happens when you assume" Alexis laughed.

"No, it's just, where is she? Does she live close? Why don't you talk to her anymore? I just ask because my mom is my best friend and I couldn't imagine living without her" he said.

"We are estranged and she lives in the city here" Alexis said flatly and with an 'I don't want to talk about this' tone.

"It's cool. I was just curious is all" he said looking sheepish. They rode the rest of the way to the house in silence. When they arrived at the house, Alexis dropped her stuff on her desk and ran to the restroom. She'd had to pee since the voodoo lady's house so she couldn't hold it any longer. When she came out, people were looking at her but trying not to. They would glance and then put their noses deep in their files. She wondered what was going on. Did she have toilet paper stuck to her heel or hanging out of the top of her skirt? When she got back to her desk even Rodriguez looked like she'd kicked his puppy. Her Lieutenant came out and yelled for Alexis to come into his office. 'Great' she thought to herself. 'What now?'

"Fleece, I have some bad news for you" he said gently.

"What? Spit it out already!" she said.

"We just got a 10-57 (missing person) over the radio" he said looking at her pointedly.

"So, let's go. Who is it?" she asked.

"Your mother, Alexis" he said and slumped back into his chair. Alexis, too slumped down in her chair. She had not spoken with her mother for several years but then this happens. She has to work the case. "I'm giving the case to Rodriguez and Perez" he said.

"The hell you are! Rodriguez and I are more than capable of working this case" she protested.

"You're too close to the case" he argued.

"All the more reason I should be on the case. I can help with details. Look, either you give me the case officially or I'll take it on unofficially" she said to test him.

"Fine. You and your partner can have the case but I'm keeping a close eye on you both" he said rising from his desk, a sign she was dismissed. She left his office, grabbed her jacket and motioned for Rodriguez to follow her. He looked at the Lieutenant for approval who nodded. Rodriguez picked up the pace behind Alexis like a tag-a-long little brother.

"Where are we going?" Rodriguez asked.

"I figured we'd start with her place first."

"I thought you were estranged" he said confused.

"We were but I still kept tabs on her" Alexis smiled a sheepish grin.

"You devil. Did she know?" he asked.

"Nope. I was slick" she said.

"Sounds like it" he said in amazement. They arrived to the little house her mother had rented on West 65th Street near Detroit and the new Gordon Square Arts District. She had lived in that house even when Alexis was a teenager so she was able to find it easily.

They searched the house from top to bottom and found nothing that would indicated she'd been taken. Everything was neat and in order but one door remained closed. Alexis opened the door to what used to be her bedroom and found it to be a shrine. It was just as she had left it when she left to get her own apartment just before signing up for the police academy. She had been working two jobs at the time to pay rent and taking her classes in the evenings just to make everything work and to avoid having to live at home any longer than she needed. He mother was bipolar with violent mood swings and anxiety. At that time, people didn't take medication so she was unpredictable from minute to minute. Alexis was afraid to have friends over for fear of embarrassment. He mother knew everything and no one else was ever right. She always complained about how bad she had things and how Alexis should be grateful for the things she had. She was expected to be seen, not heard, like the old saying but it went all the way into her teenage years. Alexis was not allowed to have an opinion or dislike something her mother liked. All these things came rushing back to her as she stood in the doorway to her room looking around. These had not been happy childhood days but she didn't know that until she was older. She thought everybody lived the same way.

As she started to close her door, Alexis noticed something on the mirror of her dresser. Her mother had pinned up all the newspaper articles about her daughter around the edges of the mirror but in the center, in red lipstick were the words "You know where to find us!" Alexis stepped out of the room and ordered it a crime scene so they could analyze the lipstick, dust for prints, etc.

"Now what? Where are you going to find them?" Rodriguez asked.

"I think I know exactly where they are" she said. Next she spoke into her walkie, "Badge # 38135 is 10-49 proceed to Capitol Theater on W.65th North of Detroit."

"The theater?" he asked.

"She used to take me there as a child to watch movies. It was cheap on the weekends and since I didn't really have any friends, she and I would go to the theater to see movies. It's been abandoned for years though" Alexis explained.

When they arrived, the front doors were unchained, just waiting for them to come in. Alexis went down to the stage and Rodriguez went up to the projector's booth. Alexis found her mom immediately tied to a double ended rigging. She searched her body and found teeth marks on her mom's wrists. *'This bastard just thinks he can drink from everybody'* Alexis thought to herself. She tried to untie her mom but before she could she was hoisted up into the air and hung from her wrists, screaming out Alexis' name. Then came the voice:

"Awwwww. Alexis. Can't save mommy can we?" came the very feminine voice. Stunned by the gender of the voice Alexis countered:

"A little dramatic don't you think?" An evil laugh came from the female voice. "Why don't you show yourself and let us settle this like ladies?" Alexis suggested.

"Because you are no match for me. I am much stronger than you and it would just be a bloodbath" the voice chuckled.

"Why don't you let me be the judge of that?"

"Awwwwww. Detective Alexis Fleece. Always got something to prove" the voice said sarcastically.

"Being a woman Detective isn't easy" Alexis said defensively. There was a strong wind from the rafters, a black hooded creature who flew back up just as fast and left a small slice on the left side of Alexis' neck. "What are you?" Alexis demanded.

"I am a vampire. A very old, wise and strong vampire who would best you on my worst day" she gloated.

"Let's find out. Stop playing shadow games" Alexis demanded.

A dark hooded creature descended from the rafters onto the middle of the stage. Alexis took out her gun and fired several shots at the being before realizing they were making no difference. The being took her cloak off and revealed a stunning body dressed in red vinyl from head to toe with a red mask and long raven hair that fell from the back of the mask to her waist. She had a whip attached to her side and she took it out and cracked it on stage a few times just for effect. As Alexis moved towards her, the vampire slung this whip around Alexis' neck and pulled her to her. She grabbed her around her mid-section as well and licked the side of her neck that had been sliced open.

"Mmmmmm. You taste good. Taste like fear and rage mixed together" the vampire said. Alexis struggled to get out from the whip to no avail. "You cannot get away from me" she said. Alexis reached up and punched the vampire in the side of the head which made her grip on the whip loose enough for just one second to allow Alexis to escape.

"You're not all that scary" Alexis said huffing and puffing. She lurched towards the vampire, grabbing the whip on the way and landed on top of her on the ground. Alexis punched, kicked, yelled and did whatever she could to attempt to maim this vampire. Finally, the vampire had enough, grabbed Alexis' mother and flew off into the rafters, refusing Alexis' personal, verbal attacks.

Alexis left the theater feeling defeated. Marty was waiting outside for her.

"Where were you?" she accused.

"I was watching the entrance in case she tried to get away."

"Well, she did and she took my mother with her again. Thanks for all your help" Alexis scoffed, walked to the car and waited for him to make his way back. They drove back to the house in silence.

Chapter Eleven: The Informant

That night, Alexis took a long, hot bubble bath, thinking about the day's events. Not only was it a vampire, but a female vampire and it was after her. What had she done? How had she wronged this vampire that she went through such an extensive plan to get to her? Had she killed a former lover of the vampire? She didn't even know how to kill vampires so that couldn't be it. Unless the lover had been a human. Hmmmmm. That was an interesting thought. But she'd only killed three people in her entire time on the force. The first was a man who was beating his wife and children on a domestic call and when they arrived he came out of the back room with a gun. The second was unfortunately a kid in an alley she was patrolling before she made Detective and the kid pulled a gun on her so she shot him. The third was a complete accident. They were going after a supposed female vampire drug kingpin and there were guns everywhere. She reached for one and fired but another woman stepped in front of her, taking the bullet for her. Could it be this woman who was the vampire's lover? Could it be they were lesbians? Alexis didn't know much about same sex relationships and how it worked or if it was the same as 'regular' relationships. She didn't understand the degree of love for the other person is the same as a 'regular' relationship. She didn't understand all their protesting and equal rights stuff. She didn't understand if it was something you grew into, was social or were born that way. She knew very little. She called her friend Whitney whom she had an inkling was gay to see if they could have lunch on Sunday so she could explain it to her. Whitney was more than happy to oblige and confirmed that she was gay.

At lunch, Whitney set Alexis straight with all the information she needed to understand the bond that the vampire and the victim, Lavina had together but she'd thought Lavina was human. "Maybe the vampire turned Lavina when I shot her to save her life" Alexis said aloud.

Monday, Alexis dug out the old case file for Lavina and did some digging. Granted it was old and most peoples' memories from that time were pretty far gone but there was one man, from the old cartel, still in prison, that she could talk to on the phone. He said he knew Lavina was involved with this other woman though the vampire king pin was in love with her. He said it used to infuriate his boss and he threatened the life of this woman many times but Lavina wouldn't give her up to him. He said on the night of the shooting, he didn't think Lavina was taking a bullet for him but covering her lover. The vampire was so upset when Lavina was shot that he turned her into a vampire so they could be together.

The pieces were coming together so she redid her suspect board and stood there looking at it for over 30 minutes. That's where Rodriguez found her when he arrived for work.

"Running a little late today, I see" she said to him.

"You know how it is with kids. None are ready at the same time" he complained. He took a walk over to the suspect board and stood there looking at it with Alexis for about 10 minutes before he said anything.

"Are you sure about this?" he asked.

"Right as rain" she declared.

"Ok. So, how do we fight this monster?"

"That's the part I'm still working on" Alexis admitted.

Chapter Twelve: The Private Investigator

Alexis sat waiting in a small bar in Lakewood called Around the Corner in hopes no one would recognize her. She sat there in her jogging suit with her hair tied up in a ponytail and her feet up on the chair next to her. She had a beer in front of her which she was slowly working on as she wanted to be as clear headed as possible for this meeting. He walked in and headed directly to her table. Straight out of the 1950's Detective comic books; trench coat, hat and sneaky looking. Alexis couldn't help but snicker when she saw him. He ordered a scotch on the rocks, pulled out his paper and pen and asked:

"So, Ms. Fleece, why am I here?"

"I need you to track someone down for me" she said sheepishly.

"You're a Detective. Do you usually do that?" he sneered.

"Yes but this one is personal and I need it done fast, faster that our burecratic red tape will allow us" she replied.

"I see. So, who is this person, where can I find them and how do you know them?"

"Well, she is a vampire, I don't know where she sleeps and she's after me so I'd like to catch her while she's out for the night and lay a trap."

"A vampire? Really?" he asked and started to get up from the table.

"I know it sounds a little weird but I have proof she exists and is after me. Please find her" Alexis pleaded. He was a big softy for beautiful women so he agreed to the case.

"Any idea where I might find her?"

"Some place dark during the day as they can't be exposed to uv lights".

"Okay. I'll see what I can dig up. Get it?" he asked as he laughed to himself.

"Thanks for your belief in me and please be discreet" she said. She told him about the old sting operation and he took notes feverishly.

"No problem" he said standing, after making some more notes, downed his drink in one gulp and left the bar in a flash. Alexis couldn't believe she was actually doing this. She was the Detective and she was handing the investigation over to a Private Investigator (PI) for the first time in her career.

That night after her shift, she went home and sank into bed joyously. Rodriguez had been asking her all day if she was okay. She worried about the PI and her heart just wasn't into her work today. She wanted the vampire found so her second plan could be put into motion. She tried reading while in bed but she fell right asleep and woke up when her alarm went off the next morning. 'Wow, haven't slept like that in months' she said to herself. She agreed that it was the pressure of the PI that made things alright.

Later that afternoon she had a meeting with the PI who had called her at the station that morning and said they needed to speak. She made an excuse to get away and headed back to where she met him the day before.

"I'm surprised you're calling me back so soon."

"Well, it was a very easy case so I won't charge you my full going rate" he joked.

"Thanks" she said flatly, "Now what did you find?"

"Well, your assessment of Lavina was incorrect. She was not trying to duck out of the way but she was in love with two men. A vampire man. This man, after the shooting swooped her away to God knows where and turned her into a vampire herself. Consequently the police never found her body and the vampire kingpin turned her after they were safe. Lavina had come clean to him afterwards, including telling him she was in love with the other woman. She had taken that bullet to save her life but in doing so, she wrecked her possible life with her by having to spend her fledgling years with the vampire man. He left her after her "probation" period was over and they've never been close since. Seems like he broke a promise to her or something. That part is still unclear as of yet. Lavina's female lover was found dead a couple years ago when she had mysteriously drowned in a creek in West Virginia. There is no further information on her death but police suspected foul play."

"Wow! That's good work Detective" Alexis said.

"Do you want to hear the kicker?"

"Absolutely."

"The vampire kingpin is someone you know and trust, right here in your backyard."

"Rodriguez?" Alexis asked but already knew the answer.

"Boy, you're quick. Like I said, this was a 'quickie' of sorts so I'll only charge you half." Alexis slid the money filled envelope across the table to him and sat there staring into space. The PI got up and left, leaving her sitting there still staring off into space. She was putting things together in her head. His reluctance to show up on night calls, his cold skin and touch, his keeping close to the case, all made sense now. How could she have not known it was him? She'd been undercover and with him personally for quite some time. 'Makeup' was the only explanation she could come up with. Presently, she had to weigh her options here. She knew very little about vampires and how to kill them so she went home, called in sick for the rest of the day and got online. She concluded the best ways to kill a vampire were:

- Fire
- Decapitation
- Stake through the heart
- Holy water
- Giving them something tedious to count (like grains of sand or rice, etc.) which would distract them so she could perform one of the other ways of killing them

She immediately ran out to the local pawn shop on Lorain Ave and W.114, where she knew she would find what she was looking for.

"I'm looking for daggers" she told the pawn broker.

"What kind?"

"What do you mean? Daggers."

"Short, long, jewel encrusted, gold, silver, forged steel, etc."

"Well, I hadn't thought about that. I'm guessing the forged from silver simple ones would work just fine" she guessed.

When he came back to the counter, he had a big assortment of daggers for her to choose from. She picked an identical pair with dragon fangs encrusted on the handles. "*How fitting for what's going on*" she thought to herself. She also picked a small one to carry inside her boot next to her boot gun. Then she thought of a movie she had once seen, got a strange idea and asked the pawn broker for an uncommon object.

"You got any wooden stakes back there?"

"You hunting vampires?" he laughed. Alexis gave him a stern look so he disappeared into the back of the store. About five minutes later he came back with an armful and a steel box.

"What's in the box?" she asked.

"Well, as far as I can guess, it was a vampire hunter's kit from the olden days. You know, like Van Helsing?"

"Who?" she asked to an astonished faced man. "Never mind, I'll take everything." She stuffed her findings into the duffel back she had brought with her and headed back to her apartment for closer inspection.

Chapter Thirteen: The Takedown

After she got home, she spread out all of her loot onto her kitchen table and started to examine each and every piece. It looked like all the stakes came from the same person for their name had been burned into the handle, "Selene". She wondered who that was, if it was from a movie or someone from the old days. Each stake had been carved to an exact point at the tip with no splintering, was sanded down and clear coated with enamel. She took the stakes and hid them around her house, not knowing if she'd have a fight in her home but she would be prepared for it in every room. She took the small dagger and ran her thumb down the blade quickly and cut herself. "*At least they're sharp*" she thought to herself. She bandaged her finger before inspecting the identical dragons. She just had a feeling about these two daggers. There was something that spoke to her when she looked at them.

Suddenly, there was a knock at the door that startled Alexis for she had been deep in though. She threw the daggers under the couch with the small one going into her boot. She opened the door to find Marty standing there looking drunk.

"I'm sorry for dropping by unannounced in the middle of the night like this but I just had to get away."

"Is your wife that bad?" she asked.

"Worse. She won't let me have any time with my friends. Everything has to be about her which she gets to have friends while I watch the kids. Don't get me wrong, I love my kids but sometimes it's just too much" he complained. "Do you mind if I sit down on the couch for a few minutes to cool off?"

"Well, I was expecting company" she hedged.

"It'll only be for a few minutes. I promise" he said pushing past her and sat at the other end of the couch for she had no extra chairs in her living room, something she kicked herself for now. He took a sip of the water that Alexis had provided him with and then with super speed he lunged the length of the couch and was in her lap.

"What are you doing?" Alexis asked squirming under him. He continued to try to take in her smell, (the coconut from her hair, the White Diamonds perfume she wore and the strawberry lip gloss she was always applying). "Get off of me!"

"You know you want me. I've known it since our first ride-along. The way you looked up to me in almost reverence, took notes at my every word and the playful punches in the arm you always gave me. Those are signs of a woman who's interested in a man."

"No, they're not. I was just trying to learn from you and then play around with you as any partner would" she explained. He had moved to sniffing her ear, down her neck where he lingered and into her cleavage.

"You have such great tits! I've always admired them. I know you work out, run and eat healthy but those pull down exercises have really done you breasts justice." Alexis felt like she was under a ton of bricks, unable to move and starting to suffocate. As Marty moved to straddle her, she was able to get the lift and momentum she needed to push him down on the couch and get up and run to the kitchen.

"You can't escape me Alexis Fleece. I know your every move. Hell, I gave you those moves. Now just come here and I won't hurt you" he almost sounded sincere. She remembered the daggers under the couch.

"So, we can sit on the couch and talk like real people or are you going to pounce on me again?" she asked, hoping her plan would work.

"I promise to keep my distance, besides, I have a confession." This intrigued Alexis so she agreed to come back. The two of them sat down at either ends of the couch. She waited for his move but he was took quick. He pinned her down, laying on top of her on the couch. She was able to roll him off her, onto the coffee table and grab a dagger from under the couch. She spoke as she sat on him:

"I know you were the vampire kingpin we attempted to sting all those years ago. I also know you turned Lavina, left her, killed her lover and now she's after me." He looked horrified at the dagger she had in her hand.

"If you know I am a vampire, then you should know I'd be able to do this" he said as he lunged out from under her and to her throat but he made the mistake of stopping before he bit her just to take in her scent one last time. She grabbed the dagger in her right hand and slit his throat from one side to the other.

She never saw how much blood came out of a body when their throats had been slit. She had always arrived after they'd been dead for awhile. He was squirting blood from his neck, spitting up blood and the floor around them was filling up fast with the sticky red liquid. She had to get out of there. She knew it would be a crime scene soon and she had to get her story straight for her Lieutenant. She also knew Lavina would be hunting her more now than ever since she killed her vampire Maker.

Suddenly there was a knock on the door. A shaking Alexis peeked through the keyhole and there stood her Lieutenant. She quickly opened the door and he burst in.

"I see we have a problem" he sneered.

"How did you know?"

"A neighbor called about the commotion. Don't worry about a thing. I'll get this taken care of for you." Just then, in walked a young man in a police officer's uniform and the Lieutenant seemed like he'd expected him. The Officer took one look at Alexis and she swore he was seeing stars. "Alexis?" he said pulling her attention back to him, "This is officer Skendar. You are going to be staying with him until this thing is resolved. Pack some things as you won't be able to return to your apartment for a while and get a move on" he instructed her. Alexis was stunned. 'She couldn't return'? What was she going to do? Just live with this guy she's never met?

"Move it!" he barked at her. She turned into survival mode and ran into the bedroom and started packing. It only took her about ten minutes and she was back in the living room with her two bags. The young officer took them from her and motioned for her to follow him. She took one last look at her apartment when she reached the door and then followed Skendar down to the waiting car.

Chapter Fourteen: The Connection He Was Looking For

She didn't say a word on the entire ride to his house. When they arrived, he carried her bags inside and she followed him through the house as he gave her instructions. Lastly, he took her to her bedroom, placed her bags next to her bed and left her to herself. She flopped down onto the bed and started balling her eyes out into the pillow silently. He stood outside her door and heard her cries. He'd felt sad for her, she wasn't like most humans to him. She seemed genuine and he'd hated that she'd got messed up in this thing with Lavina. Plus, could she be the woman from his dream? She fit the description and the moment he laid eyes on her, he felt something rumble inside him, something he hadn't felt since Isabella. Could it be?

Alexis never got up the next day. She slept until the evening. When she came out of her room, Skendar was sitting in the living room on his laptop. He looked up when she came in.

"Are you hungry? I went to the grocery store but didn't know what you liked so I picked up some lunch meat, cheese and bread for sandwiches. I already ate but I'd be willing to make you one if you' like." She just nodded her head 'no' and went back into her room and into the bathroom to take a long hot shower. She ended up curled up in a ball, sitting in the tub under the hot running water and crying. Afterwards, she locked herself in her bedroom for two more days.

Finally, Skendar had enough. He knocked on her door one evening and spoke to her through it.

"Hello? You really should eat something. Besides, I have two tickets to The Devices and I'd like for you to go with me tonight." There was a long pause on the other side of the door before she cracked it to look at him.

"The Devices?" she asked in a childlike tone.

"Yes" he said knowing full well that they were her favorite band.

"Well, I suppose getting out might help. What time?"

"Show starts at 8pm."

"Okay. Thanks" she said before closing the door between them. He thought it went well. She needed to get out and he wanted to get to know her better anyway and this would be a great start.

The show was loud but Alexis seemed to be having a good time to Skendar. With their mechanical metal sound, Alexis was smiling and banging her head to the music. The band played for two hours and by the end of the night, both of their ears were ringing which made conversation on the drive home nearly impossible. On the way inside, Skendar mentioned that he had a bottle of wine in the fridge and she jumped at the chance of some alcohol.

They sat in the living room, lounging on the comfy overstuffed couch, drinking and talking the night away. Reluctantly, Skendar excused himself right before dawn but Alexis passed out on the couch after finishing off the second bottle of Ice Wine. When she woke the next evening, Skendar was sitting across from her on his laptop again.

"Sorry. Was I drooling?" she asked.

"No. You slept like an angel." She hesitated for a moment before asking:

"So, when do we get back on the vampire case?"

"I'm not sure" he lied, knowing full well her Lieutenant pulled her off the case due to her involvement in it.

"Well, I'm going to call my Lieutenant tonight and ask him."

"Why don't you take some more time? I don't mind having you here. You've been great and I'd hate to lose you."

"Thanks but I've imposed long enough. I need to go back to my apartment and crack this case. Do you know, that I've only not solved three of my cases in the past five years?"

"That's impressive. I hope to be as good as you one day" he said humbly.

"You will. It comes with time and experience. Now, where's my cell phone?" she asked looking around.

"I dunno. I didn't see you bring one with you when you came" he said hopefully.

"Oh, that's right. It's on the charger in my room. I'm so forgetful sometimes" she laughed and went off to call in. When she returned, he could see she was in a foul mood.

"What's wrong?"

"They pulled me from MY case!" she yelled. "Can you believe it?" she demanded.

"Yes, I just got the call from my Lieutenant and he said the same thing. I'm so sorry Alexis" he apologized. Now it was her time to be sorry.

"No, I'm sorry. I'm sorry you got dragged into this."

"It's alright.

"What are you going to do? I know you have something planned already by the look on your face."

"Well, I keep copies of all my files online so I'm going to review them and start from scratch."

"I thought you said you knew Lavina was behind all this."

"She is but how do I catch her?" She stopped for a moment, frozen in time, then said, "Now I need to think like a vampire. Got any ideas?" She startled him. He'd never heard anyone want to do anything like a vampire. Vampires had always been the monstrous creatures of the night. People feared them but this little woman seemed afraid of nothing. He'd done some of his own research on Lavina and had a few leads but he needed to play them low and lead Alexis to Lavina on her own.

"Well…" he said pulling his laptop closer, "I've been doing some research on vampires and there's tons of myths circulating out there so I just have to figure out what's true and what's myth."

"I know, I know…they only come out at night, they drink blood, human bullets can't kill them, they have no reflection, silver can kill them, wooden stakes are not their friends, they don't eat and they catch fire in the sunlight, blah blah blah." He was amazed at her knowledge of the undead and stared at her blankly. "I've watched a few vampire movies in my life. I especially love Lost Boys, you know, before vampires sparkled." He laughed at this for that concept truly was ridiculous and whomever came up with that should be shot.

"I do have some leads if you want to hear them?" he offered. She quickly sat down on the couch staring intently at him. She was intrigued by more than a little.

"Sure! What do you have?"

"Well, there's this vampire club in the flats. I'm sure it's full of pretenders but we could do some asking around and maybe find something…" Alexis jumped up and grabbed her coat before he could say another word. "Where are you going?"

"You show me…to the club genius."

All the way there, Alexis peppered Skendar with questions about vampires. He tried to help, without giving away too much or himself in the process. He explained that any vampire as brazen to go around killing humans and leaving their bodies for humans to find is not only a sociopath but one addicted to power and those in power all hung around together. So, if they could find the owner of the bar, get into their circles, then they'd have a better chance at finding Lavina. She seemed impressed with the idea. Now he just had to hope he didn't run into anyone who knew him.

When they arrived, he suggested he do all the talking since he'd done most of the 'research'. She reluctantly agreed but wanted to be there to hear everything. He also reluctantly agreed but knew there'd come a time he couldn't hold up to his end of the bargain if he came across someone he knew. When they got to the club doors, he used his mind control powers on the doorman and they got let in easily enough. They went directly to the bar and ordered drinks, she a Patron Café and he a 1912 Merlot. As they sat at the bar looking around and sipping their drinks, they quietly discussed the people around them, trying to decide which people were pretenders and which were the real deal. Skendar purposely secretly picked out a pretender, said he looked 'legit' so they made their way over to him. They started slow dancing on the floor next to him before making conversation.

"This is a great club" Skendar yelled above the music and loud enough for the man to hear.

"Yes. It's great but too many pretenders here" she chimed back.

"Hey lady. Not everyone is a pretender here" the man interrupted them. They stopped dancing and turned to him.

"Really?" she asked, seeming to be enthralled.

"Yes. The owner and staff are all real vampires. They've modeled this club after a well-known vampire club in Romania down to the light fixtures" he said proudly.

"Really? Have you ever been there?" Alexis asked.

"No but I read about it online."

"Oh, online" Alexis said and turned to Skendar, putting her back to the man purposely.

"Hey, it's true" he said turning her around. "I know the owner and she's really cool" he protested.

"I'm sure you do pal" Skendar said attempting to walk away. The man grabbed his wrist.

"Look, I can introduce you to her if you don't believe me." Alexis and Skendar looked at each other, disbelieving it could be this easy.

"Okay man. Bring her to the bar and we'll buy her a drink" Skendar said.

"Silly man. Vampires don't drink human alcohol…only blood but I'll bring her to tell you herself" and with that the man disappeared into the blackness. Alexis and Skendar headed back to their seats at the bar but before long a tall, beautifully ivory skinned woman appeared next to them.

"So…you two are not believers I'm told." The words flowed sweetly from between her rosy red lips.

"I'm sorry to offend you in your place of business…" Alexis said before being cut off by the woman.

"Ahhhhh…I am right then young one" she said stroking Alexis' hair that fell down her back.

"We do not mean to offend you, it's just that we've been to many vampire clubs in Romania and this doesn't resemble any that we know of" Skendar chimed in. She turned to look at him and was taken aback by his beauty yet she did not outwardly recognize him as another vampire. 'Her powers are weak' he thought to himself after looking inside her but he knew she hung around with the crowd they were looking for.

"This is a very old underground club, I'm sure you've never been there. It's very elite" she continued.

"That must be it. So, tell me more about yourself" he said pulling up a chair for the woman between him and Alexis.

"Oh, we vampires are very secretive."

"I know but we are lovers of the dark ones."

"Well, in that case, I am Tonya, I am only 10 years old, born again in Romania from one of the oldest vampires alive, Lavina and I love long walks on the beach" she mocked them. Alexis and Skendar perked up at the name but tried to play it cool. How awesome was it that their first club brought them to this woman and possibly the vampire they are hunting.

"Lavina? Never heard of her" Alexis said nonchalantly.

"Really? Lovers of dark ones and never heard of Lavina? She's amazing! She was once a ruthless killer but has since calmed down after her latest lover was killed. It really took a toll on her and she's never been the same since. I'd been her familiar after her lover's death and consoled her so she turned me as she enjoyed my company. We were lovers for a while, up until she found HIM." She looked away with tears in her eyes.

"I'm so sorry" Alexis reached for her hand but the woman pulled away before she could touch it.

"Thank you but we've just recently come back in contact as she's moved to the states to start a new life." Skendar secretly nodded at Alexis who caught the small gesture but thankfully the woman did not.

"I'd like to meet this wonderful woman who created such a beautiful creature as yourself. She must be amazing" Skendar coaxed her.

"Oh, she is! Maybe I'll bring you as my date to the Halloween Ball next week."

"That'd be great!" Alexis said.

"I'm sorry honey. I meant just him. Three's a crowd you know" she said getting up to leave. Alexis was obviously perturbed but Skendar continued the game.

"I'd love that. How will you find me?" he asked.

"Silly. I don't 'find' people, that's a vampire myth, you'll just meet me here at 9pm on Halloween. Dress like Dracula, it'll be fun" she said and disappeared into the crowd. When she was out of earshot Alexis grabbed him by the arm and nearly ripped it off tugging on him.

"You are not going to that party without me!"

"Looks like we don't have a choice" he smiled.

"You are not an undercover Detective. You are a damn rookie officer! You can't do this!"

"This may be our only option to find this Lavina so I have to go. You do want to find her don't you?"

"Yes but…"

"There's no 'but's', it's settled. I'm going."

CHAPTER Fifteen: The Halloween Party

As Skendar got ready, Alexis went over and over police procedure so he wouldn't do something wrong to get Lavina off on a technicality. She gave him a pair of glasses, with a small camera on the bridge of the nose. She then put a tack pin on the collar of his shirt that was part of his Dracula costume so she could hear everything that happened. She reassured him that she would be in a black van outside, waiting to follow him to the party.

At 9pm sharp, Skendar was at the club, sitting at the bar, waiting for his mystery woman and the Halloween party. At 9:10pm, she touched his shoulder seductively and he nearly jumped out of his skin. She smiled a toothy smile and motioned for him to follow her into the back room. She was dressed as Frankenstein's bride with the large hair, pale skin which came naturally and a long black, tight fitting dress. Skendar thought she looked amazing and happily followed her.

"This is a huge event" she said pushing him down onto the couch in her office. "They only do it on Halloween and everybody in the vampire community will be there so please do not embarrass me" she instructed him with a very serious tone. "I don't usually take humans to the party with me but you are just so damned sexy that I couldn't resist you" she said sitting down on the couch very close to him. She leaned over and kissed his ear and moved down his neck and eventually landed on his plush lips. She kissed him very seductively and he started to feel the arousal in his pants. She broke the kiss, looked down and seemed pleased. "Okay, it's time to go. The party starts at 10:00pm and it's a 20 minute drive to get to the location." She stood, flattened down her dress and held out her hand to help him up off the couch.

Alexis was sitting outside in her black van, listening and watching his every movement. She found herself feeling a little jealous when the woman kissed him, surprising herself for she hadn't thought of him that way until just now. When the van moved with him in it, she instructed her driver to follow him, not too closely and try to be undercover without detection by the woman.

Skendar found himself in a limousine and the woman sat awfully close to him.

"It just occurred to me that I don't even know your name" he said.

"Oh" she laughed. "It's Jodina. That might be important" she smiled at him.

After 20 minutes, they arrived at a large house with large pillars on the front of the house, a large upper balcony, and plush gardens with a fountain at the entrance making a roundabout for drop-off. She motioned for him to get out of the car first and then she made her exit. She took his arm and they walked into the foray of the house. They were immediately greeted by a maid with a tray of champagne glasses with a red liquid in them.

"The ones on the left are blood for us and the ones on the right are a 1912 Merlot for you. Take one to take away your inhibitions as it's very strong but don't drink too many because I don't want you drunk" she instructed him. He took the drink and started sipping it and she was right, it was very strong even for human alcohol. He followed her through the house and into the back where there was a pool, large tables for sitting but most people were standing around and in their costumes which Skendar found amusing. She took him over to a very slender, sexy and attractive woman.

"Skendar, this is the host of our party, Lavina."

"Pleased to meet you" he said, extending his hand. She took it sideways, indicating she wanted him to kiss the top of it which he did.

"Jodina, a human, really?"

"He's a special human, very attractive" Jodina explained defensively.

"I can see that. May I taste him later?" Lavina asked.

"You may do as you wish. It is your party after all."

"That pleases me greatly." She then turned to Skendar. "Have you ever been tasted by a vampire?"

"No" he lied.

"Excellent! I love the first taste of a human" she said excitedly.

"As you wish" he said, knowing he was going to be found out when she tasted him. He started devising a plan in his head to avoid her bite. Lavina then turned to a waiting couple and greeted them.

"That's all for now" Jodina said to Skendar and lead him to another couple near the pool and introduced him to them but he barely heard what she said as he was still devising his plan in his head. He was on his own to decide what to do.

As the night went on, dread encompassed him. What was he going to do? Should he skip out of the party without Jodina knowing? Then he might never get a chance at Lavina again. Eventually, around 1am, Lavina tracked him down, took him by the hand, lead him into the house and to an upstairs bedroom. Once inside, she locked the door and pushed him down on the bed. She took off his pants which caught him unexpectedly. She stripped out of her slinky dress and lay down on the bed next to him. She started kissing him and stroking him. It took all the control in the world for him not to get aroused. He could tell she was getting frustrated with him.

"What's wrong?" she asked pouting.

"I guess I had too much to drink tonight."

"Oh" she said disappointed. "Guess we'll have to save this for another night then when you're sober. I don't want to drink from someone who's had as much alcohol as you apparently drank." With that, she got up, got dressed and left the room. The amount of relief that he felt was overwhelming. His lack of a plan hadn't mattered and he'd thought quick on his feet though he had to use a huge amount of control. He got up, got dressed and headed down to find Jodina.

"So, I hear it didn't go well" she said accusingly. "I told you not to embarrass me."

"I'm sorry dear."

"I told you not to drink a lot" she accused him.

"Guess I was nervous and couldn't help it." Jodina grabbed him by the hand and lead him to the waiting limo. He checked for Alexis and the black mobile van and sure enough it was waiting outside just down the street. Jodina took him back to the club and into her office.

"Luckily for you, Lavina wants to set up another meeting with you. She gets rather obsessed with people easily and you seem to be her latest catch. I'll call you when she lets me know when that is. Write down your phone number and you may leave, for now." Skendar quickly wrote down him number on the pad of paper on her desk and practically ran out of the club and into the Alexis' van.

"Did you have fun tonight?" she accused.

"Didn't you hear me? I got to meet Lavina and she wants me back. That works out well for us. We can sting her the next time around."

"Sting her? You've been watching too many movies. You did do the right thing with her I guess."

"Why are you distressed?"

"I dunno. I guess I didn't expect her to seduce you."

"Was that a problem?" he asked curiously.

"No" she said quickly. A little too quickly which he picked up on. '*Has she developed feelings for me*?' he wondered to himself.

"Well, we better get going. I have a lot of tape to go through from tonight. I'll be up until the wee hours of the night" she commented. He smiled as she told the driver to take them home. When they got home, she immediately locked herself into her bedroom and started going through the tapes. This left him to get comfy on the couch and wonder what was going on with Alexis and replay the events of the night in his head.

Chapter Sixteen: The Sting

A week later, Skendar got the much anticipated call from Jodina. She said Lavina wanted to meet in a week on a Saturday. He informed Alexis immediately and she started her plan, recruiting several of her fellow Detectives to quietly help her on the case. With Skendar's help, she laid out a blueprint of Lavina's house in order for the entrance to her house for the Detectives. All of them listened to the tape and trained Skendar in police procedures for a take-down of a murder suspect. The Detectives convinced a Judge to give them a warrant so they could legally gain entrance to the house and use Skendar as an informant in order to get a conviction.

It was Saturday night and Alexis and Skendar were a ball of nerves.

"Remember, we need Lavina to confess to you that she committed the murders."

"I know. I'll get her to do it. Don't worry" Skendar encouraged her. Her fellow Detectives placed the earpiece microphone and camera glasses on him and put him in a rented car and sent him off to Lavina's house.

Precisely at 10pm, Skendar rang the doorbell to Lavina's house and was greeted by a young male who took his coat and directed him to her parlor where he would wait for Lavina. He didn't have to wait long as she appeared in the doorway in a purple lace baby doll teddy staring lustfully at him. She came in and sat down on his lap.

"How are you tonight my dear?" she purred and batted her eyes at him.

"Anxious" he replied.

"Me too. I have been waiting impatiently for your blood and I'm not going to wait any longer." She placed a kiss on his lips and then led him upstairs into the bedroom where she again locked the door behind her. She took off his clothes, pushed him down on the bed roughly and climbed on top of him where she straddled his hips. She could see he was obviously aroused and a smile came across her face. She leaned down, kissed him on the lips and then moved to his ear and down his neck. She kissed, licked, nibbled and finally dug her fangs into his neck and started to drink from him. She immediately jumped off him and onto the bed next to him.

"You're a vampire!" she hissed. "I could taste it in your blood." Alexis, in the van parked outside, listening to the exchange almost fell off her chair at the accusation. She was anxious to hear his response.

"So what if I am?" he asked defiantly. Alexis was shocked at the revelation. She'd had no idea and she was usually a good judge of character due to her Detective training. Her fellow Detectives glared at her with gaping mouths and were obviously unhappy. She shrugged them off and went back to the camera screen and listening into the conversation intently.

"You mislead Jodina and myself intentionally."

"I wanted to meet you. I'd heard such great things about your beauty that I wanted to meet you in person."

"So you used Jodina? I like a cunning man" she purred.

"Have you ever tasted vampire blood?"

"Well…no."

"It's better than you think. It's very erotic, sensual and extra special" he encouraged her.

"I guess I'll have to try it then" Lavina said moving back towards him and sinking her fangs into his neck. He had been right in that it tasted better than any human Lavina had ever tasted. When she was done, she lay down on the bed next to him, appearing exhausted and breathing hard.

"So…what's with you and Alexis Fleece?" he asked casually. She propped herself up on one arm to look directly at him.

"How do you know about Alexis?"

"Jodina told me about your latest obsession with her. I read in the paper about the murders where all the blood had been exsanguinated from the victims and connected the dots" he said trying to sound casual.

"You are right. I drained all those people. They were people that she let go free due to her heated temper. They deserved to die and she deserved to pay for what she did to me."

"What did she do to you?"

"She tried to kill my lover a few years back in a police sting operation. I took the bullet and was then turned into a vampire to have my life saved. My Maker left me after my probation period after a disagreement but I still had my lover. She turned up dead a few years ago and I never recovered. She deserves to die next." This was all the detectives needed and moved in to take her into custody. Alexis stayed in the van as since she was on suspension, she could get the case thrown out of court on a technicality if she arrested Lavina. The police kicked down the bedroom door and quickly grabbed Lavina, threw her to the ground and handcuffed her. Skendar grabbed his clothes and dressed in record time to avoid embarrassment by the Detectives. They escorted her to a waiting undercover police car, read her the Miranda rights and took her to jail where she remained in cuffs in the cell.

When Skendar came out and to the van, Alexis came out with tempers flaring. She immediately walked up to him and slapped him across the face.

"What was that for?" he asked rubbing the side of his face.

"You didn't tell me you were a vampire" she accused.

"You didn't ask."

"Don't be coy with me. Why didn't you tell me?"

"I didn't want to scare you off when you came to stay with me."

"Well...it wasn't right" she said storming away to talk to one of the Detectives. Skendar felt crushed. He had come to realize she was the woman of his dream from so long ago and now he probably ruined it. What was he thinking revealing that? He hadn't had a choice as Lavina could taste it on him. Oh well, whatever happened, he couldn't worry about it now. He had a trial to prepare for.

As he walked off into the night his cell phone rang. It was his Lieutenant. He was permanently put on suspension upon further investigation. 'Great! What did that mean?' he wondered to himself as he headed for home.

Chapter Seventeen: The Pre-Trial

When Lavina was in court for arraignment in the evening, the Judge was rather perplexed.

"Your Honor, we move for an evening trial as my client is a vampire and cannot be out in the sunlight without drastic repercussions to her health and she has civil rights" the Defense attorney started. The Judge debated for a few moments before speaking.

"While this is a highly unlikely case and I don't usually hold court at night, you are right. The Defendant does have civil rights in our justice system and I'm required by law to obey them. Obviously, she has a right to a trial by her peers but I don't believe that today's vampires would want to be recognized or put through the media circus this is going to create. Therefore, I move to continue this matter in the evenings to a closed courtroom, meaning no reporters or cameras. Due to the highly sensitive nature of this case, jury selection will begin next week on Monday with the trial to start immediately when the selection process is completed. The Defendant will remain in custody as I don't feel she will follow the laws of this court, it's obvious that she can't follow the laws of society so bail is denied. She will remain in solitary confinement to keep her in the dark and away from the general population. It is so ordered by the court" she said, banging her gavel on the desk. She got up from behind the bench and left the courtroom shaking her head side to side.

Lavina, still handcuffed, was taken from the courtroom and returned to the downtown Justice Center jail. Alexis and Skendar had been in the courtroom to witness the proceedings yet they didn't sit together as Alexis still was not speaking to him. They were both pleased with the results. He so that he could attend the proceedings at night and so he would be able to testify against her and Alexis for she had got the result she wanted. She had relied on the justice system and it seemed to be paying off for her so far.

The following week, the jury selection process began. Both the Defense Attorney and Prosecutor were present and able to ask their own questions of the potential jurors. The first question each person was asked is if they had anything against vampires. They were amazed at the overwhelming support of vampires that the people portrayed. Then they asked if they were death-qualified, meaning against the death penalty. Any juror that was against it was removed by the Prosecutor immediately as he was going for the death penalty since Lavina had caused so many deaths herself. Have you ever been convicted of a crime, have you ever been personally defended or prosecuted by the attorneys on the case, can you be fair and impartial disregarding your personal beliefs and what amount of information do you already know about this case were some of the other questions asked to potential jurors. In the end, twelve jurors with three alternates were selected.

Lavina paced her dark cell almost every hour of every day for she had nothing else to do and couldn't sleep as vampires didn't need sleep. She was starting to feel weak as she couldn't feed. She met several times with her lawyer and that was the only time she was allowed out of her cell. She had to meet him behind glass and speak into a phone on the wall with him. She was given a private room to do so and the first thing she requested was blood so that she would be able to handle the stress and pressure of a trial. The lawyer was taken aback by this request as it was something he hadn't thought about before. She mentioned that she had a familiar that lived with her that was frequently her blood source so they could contact him and they would be able to pump some blood out of him as she needed it. Luckily she only needed it about every three days instead of every day. The lawyer said he'd make a special request to the Judge for her to have what she needed. He asked detailed questions about each of her murders and the questionable behavior of Alexis Fleece though he wouldn't be able to charge her with anything since she'd already been tried for her behavior and reprimanded appropriately. He felt the details of each murder might help the case somehow. He asked for motive and her only answer was "Alexis Fleece". He informed her that they had finished with the jury process and she would be called to court soon. They disagreed about putting her on the stand but ultimately she won with wanting to testify on her own behalf. He reassured her that he would do everything in his power to not get a conviction and at least not get murder one which carried the death penalty in Ohio. He also informed her that if they got a guilty verdict that they had the right to appeal three times and surely a different Judge would overturn the ruling if found guilty the first time.

His meetings lasted hours and it was the part of the evening that Lavina looked forward to for she was getting restless in her cell. The guards wouldn't talk to her out of fear and she was the only one in the row of solitary confinement cells. She was denied basic prison rights like TV time, gym time and mess hall socializing though she doubted anyone would want to talk to her. She was wrong. The inmates were constantly talking about her, her case, what her sentence would be, how she'd be treated being a vampire and so on.

Her lawyer made an emergency appointment with the Judge and Prosecuting lawyer in her chambers.

"Your Honor. We guarantee food to all our prisoners. They are fed in the mess hall three times a day yet my client cannot eat human food and needs blood. Is there any way we can arrange for her to get blood?"

"Objection!" said the Prosecuting lawyer. The Judge paused for a moment before speaking as if considering her options.

"Overruled. You are right that we are violating her civil rights by not allowing her sustenance. However, she cannot have visitors to feed from so what do you propose?"

"She has a familiar who lives with her that was her nightly blood donor as well as his familiar duties. I've spoken with him and he would be willing to have his blood drawn by a laboratory technician every couple nights so that she can drink it and stay strong. This is going to be a long trial and she needs to be at her best." The Prosecutor kept shaking his head 'no' in disbelief.

"Okay. I'll allow it. She needs to eat and it's not like she's killing any more people to do it. Permission granted" and with that she left her chambers.

"What are you trying to pull here?" the Prosecuting lawyer asked.

"Me? Nothing. I'm just trying to get my client her basic civil rights."

"She's a vampire. She has no civil rights. Those are for humans."

"Says who? It's not in the Constitution, Bill of Rights or any other cases that have come to court. What we have here is the ability to set a precedence for future vampires that may get caught aledigly doing criminal activities. It's going to be great!" and with that he left the room, not giving the Prosecutor any time to rebut the lawyers argument.

Chapter Eighteen: Opening Statements

The following evening, Lavina was in court, behind a glass partition with both feet and wrists shackled. The jury looked tired already which was not sitting well with Alexis. Skendar was by her side on the bench and she had slowly started talking to him again though only about the trial information. She still wasn't sure how she felt about him and she had other things to concentrate on now than her feelings for a vampire. A particular vampire. A sexy vampire…one she often had pleasurable dreams about during the day while she attempted to sleep. This whole sleeping during the day thing really threw her off her schedule and she didn't like anything to throw her off. She was a very rigorous person but she kept telling herself this was for the best. Skendar on the other hand, was well aware of Alexis' dreams about him as he'd planted them there for her. He knew he wanted her so he was going to do everything in his power to get her…and he always got what he wanted.

While deep in thought, the courtroom suddenly rose to their feet and the Judge entered the courtroom.

"Mr. Rattler, what say you?" the Judge asked the Prosecutor.

"The State of Ohio is charging Ms. Lavina Miller with seven counts of first degree murder with the death penalty as a result" he said, still standing, glaring at the Defendant. Everyone then looked at the Defendant and her attorney.

"Mr. Garrison?" the Judge asked.

"Yes your Honor. As we previously stated, the defendant has plead not guilty and had no intention of changing her plea. So, let's get started and stop wasting time" he glared back at the

Prosecutor. The Judge nodded her head in agreement and then said,

"Mr. Rattler, please start with your opening statement." Mr. Rattler stood up straighter, smoothed down the front of his suit coat, picked up his notes and moved to the center podium to address the jury.

"Ladies and gentlemen of the jury. Firstly, thank you for coming to this highly irregular proceeding. While I know you are going to be tired from the attempt to adjust your sleeping schedule, please pay attention to all the evidence presented and make a rational decision for the death penalty in the end. In the early evening of August 13th, 2012, a body was found behind a bar, down an alley, completely naked and drained of all its blood. See exhibit A" he said passing photographs to the Bailiff, who passed them to the Judge and then finally to the jury. "Upon arrival of the scene, it was taped off, witnesses were interviewed and Detective Alexis Fleece was called to the scene by her superior. When she arrived, she examined the body, scoured the crime scene and logged all the evidence she found. Only days later, a woman was found in Lakewood Park, half conscious, her heart nearly drained of blood. She had a violent reaction to Ms. Fleece when she saw her though Ms. Fleece has spoken under oath and denies ever knowing the woman. Two days later, Ms. Fleece's mother's housekeeper's twin boys were killed in their very own home, both completely drained of blood. Then Ms. Fleece's grandmother was found dead in the nursing home, also completely drained of blood, and each this time there were bite marks according to the Chief Medicinal Examiner, Dr. Snow. Lastly, Ms. Fleece's mother went missing and the defendant confronted Ms. Fleece only to escape capture. Ms. Fleece hired a Personal Investigator to look into the defendant and turns out, according to his sworn statement, that the defendant had been part of a drug cartel sting years ago. She had been part of a love triangle, took a bullet for her lover, was turned into a vampire to save her life and then left by said vampire. She then lost her lover in a 'suspected foul play' drowning. She then set out on this crusade against Ms. Fleece with the help of a fellow vampire. The vampire, had been on the police force, posing as Ms. Fleece's partner, Marty Rodriguez until he was exterminated by another vampire the very night he exposed himself to Ms. Fleece and made an attempt on her life under the direct orders of the Defendant. He had owed her from a previous situation so she required him to play his part in her game of revenge against Ms. Fleece. As you can see, according to the photographs, the defendant is vicious, uncaring of today's laws and waged a vigilante style attack against one of our finest Detectives. I know, you will find the Defendant guilty and sentence her to the death penalty for her crimes." He sat down, looking exhausted. He hadn't looked at his notes once but made a very convincing statement.

"Mr. Garrison, your opening statement please?" the Judge asked. He nodded and stood up, squaring his shoulders and walked directly over to the jury box, bypassing the center podium.

"Ladies and gentlemen. If you could not see through the smoke and mirror provided to you by Mr. Rattler, my Defendant was not waging a war on Detective Fleece though she entirely deserved it. What Mr. Rattler left out of his opening statement was the botched and violent lack of case work done by Ms. Fleece. She had been reprimanded several times for her brute force and some of the cases she'd taken down were overturned due to her not following police procedure."

"Objection! Detective Fleece is not on trial here!" Mr. Rattler jumped out of his seat and bellowed.

"Maybe she should be!" Mr. Garrison fired back.

"Gentlemen!" the Judge shouted between them and gave each of them a stern looking at. "The only person on trial here is Ms. Lavina Miller. Please leave your accusations about Ms. Fleece and her work conduct to yourself as they are unimportant to the case. May the record strike any inflammatory comments about Ms. Fleece and the jury needs to disregard those same comments by Mr. Garrison" she scolded him. Mr. Garrison's shoulders shrunk and both men headed back to their tables. Alexis had been holding her breath while Garrison had been firing at her so when the Judge reprimanded him, she let out a huge sigh of relief. She's already been reprimanded for her actions and didn't want Lavina to walk because of her past but she was going to have to testify and that could open all kinds of doors she wasn't sure she was willing to walk through.

Chapter Nineteen: The Trial

It was evening two of the trial and the Defense was ordered to call their first witness. They of course called Alexis Fleece. After she was sworn in, she sat nervously in the witness box, fidgeting with her hands in her lap but trying to put on an air of confidence on her face.

"Please state your name and title for the court" Mr. Rattler started.

"Alexis Fleece, Homicide Detective for the Cleveland Police Department" she answered leaning forward to speak into the microphone.

"And how do you know the Defendant?"

"I was pursuing the drug kingpin Raphael Junior. We had found out he'd been the biggest supplier of heroin, cocaine and crystal meth in the Cleveland area. We had set up a sting where I was to go in undercover and eventually witness the purchase of a shipment by another undercover agent posing as a dealer himself. Lavina had been Raphael's 'lover' and was around on the compound all the time. I didn't 'know' her personally, that's to say we never sat down for drinks and a chat but I knew of her and her relation to Raphael."

"What happened during the sting?"

"The sting went bad. The undercover agent was supposed to shoot Raphael, as were his instructions but Lavina took the bullet for him and he got away."

"If she took a bullet, how is she still here today?"

"My sources tell me that Raphael was a vampire and instead of losing his lover, he turned the Defendant into a vampire as well. She however became later involved with my current/late partner Marty Rodriguez who she sent to kill me."

"To kill you? How did you know she sent him?"

"He told me as he attacked me."

"And how were you able to survive his attack?"

"I had got word that he was a vampire through my own private investigation. I bought silver daggers and hid them under my couch. When he came to my apartment and attacked me, I slit his throat. Immediately, my Lieutenant and another officer, Officer Skendar came bursting into my apartment and took care of him. They'd had surveillance on him and an informant had told them of his mission that night."

"Did you know this Officer Skendar prior to this evening?"

"No. He'd just been a rookie at the academy I later learned."

"That's all for now. Your witness" Mr. Rattler said to Garrison. Mr. Garrison stood, looked over his notes for a few minutes and then closely approached the witness box.

"So, Ms. Fleece. You have quite a reputation in your department, don't you?"

"I don't know what you mean."

"Surely you must. It's all over your file."

"What is?" she asked narrowing her eyes and knowing where he was going with this line of questioning.

"You're a….well….a hot head."

"Objection!" Mr. Rattler jumped up out of his seat and pounded his fist on the table.

"On what grounds?" the Judge asked.

"It's already been established that Ms. Fleece is not the one here on trial so why is he questioning her character?"

"Your Honor, it's to establish her character as part of the involvement with the sting on the defendant." Mr. Garrison countered.

"I'll allow it but you're on a very short leash Mr. Garrison" the Judge ordered.

"Thank you Your Honor. Now where was I? Oh, yes, you're a hot head."

"I don't like being called that if you don't mind" Alexis glared back at him.

"Well, it's documented that you were responsible for the release of the two victims in this case due to your inability to follow procedure."

"Well…"

"And, were you or were you not present during the sting on the Defendant? Since you were on probation at the time, all your efforts were enough to have to case dismissed against my client."

"I was not involved in the sting on your defendant. There was Officer Skendar and several other undercover officers that monitored the sting and brought in the Defendant."

"But you were there in the van, were you not?"

"I was but only as an observer."

"Is it police procedure to allow observers during sting operations?"

"Well…"

"Also, if it hadn't been for you, the first two victims in this case would have been behind bars, isn't that true?"

"So you're saying the Defendant did the public a service by killing them?"

"No, I'm just saying if it hadn't been for your temper, they wouldn't have been around for her to allegedly kill to begin with."

"Saying that were true, what about the others she 'allegedly' killed? The twins, my grandmother and my mother who is still missing? I would say she had it out for me from the beginning."

"So she's targeted you? Is that what you want the court to believe?"

"Yes. Ever since I ran the sting against Raphael, who ultimately tired of her and left her, she's had it out for me."

"Aren't we a little paranoid Ms. Fleece?"

"No, call it a cop's gut instinct and all the pieces of the puzzle put together make sense."

"And you put those pieces together yourself? How convenient. No further questions" Mr. Garrison said satisfied that he'd left doubt in the jury's mind and sat back down at his table.

"Court will be adjourned for today and will resume tomorrow morning at 9pm with the next witness for the Prosecution" the Judge ordered, banged her gavel and left the bench.

Alexis stepped down from the witness stand shaking and mad. She hadn't been so interrogated in all her life. Sure she had a few missteps in her career but she was a good Detective. She didn't take bribes, didn't look the other way, didn't let people get away with things they weren't supposed to and now she looked like some loose cannon. She was steaming by the time she reached Skendar on the bench. He attempted to put his arm around her for comfort but she just angrily shrugged him off and stormed out of the courtroom. The conversation on the ride home between them was non-existent. He didn't want to say anything else that might anger her more but there were so many things he wanted to talk to her about. Things about them. He finally decided now was not the time and when they arrived home, she rushed from the car, into her bedroom where she locked the door and lay on her bed crying hot angry tears.

Skendar sat down on his couch, going over his notes mentally for tomorrows' court appearance. He would be called as a witness and how much of his story was he willing to put out there was his biggest question. He thought and thought until his temples started to hurt and the midnight sky turned a dusky rose. He knew it was time to retire to his coffin but would he be able to rest?

The following evening, 9pm sharp, the Judge walked into the courtroom and instructed Mr. Rattler to call his next witness.

"I call Officer Skendar to the stand." Skendar was sworn in, something he'd never done and wasn't sure how he felt about it since he was an Atheist but went along with the human's procedures anyway.

"Officer Skendar, please tell us about your involvement in this case."

"Well, I was ordered by my Lieutenant to protect Ms. Fleece as he'd had several tips that her life could be in jeopardy due to the murders. I was standing outside her apartment building that night, under a tree observing when I saw Detective Rodriguez go into her apartment. I'd been told he could be part of the plan to make an attempt on Ms. Fleece's life so I followed him inside the building but stayed outside her door, listening to their conversation."

"What did you hear?"

"He told her about the Defendant and how he owed her and how Ms. Fleece's life was going to end that night. When I heard her scream, my Lieutenant had already arrived and he burst through the door only to see her lying next to him on the floor with his throat sliced from ear to ear and bleeding out. She was holding a silver dagger and shaking like a leaf. He cleaned up the mess in the apartment and instructed me to take Ms. Fleece to my apartment to 'keep an eye on her'. She was advised that she was removed from the case but she was still very upset. She and I devised a plan to catch the Defendant. She called her Detective buddies after we got our best lead, I played my part undercover with the Defendant and they made the arrest."

"Sounds simple enough."

"It was. It was actually very easy to track her down but the hardest part was to keep her from knowing I was also a vampire."

"You are a vampire too?"

"Yes. Usually we can sense it on each other, at least the stronger ones can but she could not which worked to my advantage. In the final sting, she admitted to me on video and audio that she'd had it out for Ms. Fleece and done all the killings in the area to get back at her before she ended Ms. Fleece's life as well." Mr. Rattler walked over to his desk, grabbed a video tape and popped it into the waiting VCR/TV combo next to the jury box. The courtroom sat entranced as that evenings events played out and the admission of guilt came directly from the defendant's mouth. When the undercover moved in, he turned off the tape, walked back to his table and said, "No further questions". Mr. Garrison practically jumped out of his chair at the chance to cross-examine Skendar.

"So, Officer, tell me, what's it like being a vampire?"

"Objection!" Mr. Rattler bounced out of his seat.

"It will follow a line of questioning to establish the mindset of vampires since we humans know so little about them" Mr. Garrison protested to the Judge.

"I'll allow it" she said. Mr. Garrison stood looking at Skendar, waiting for his response but when he got none he asked the questions again.

"Vampires are monsters. It's in their very nature. They have to drink blood to survive but many get their thrills from taking human lives while drinking. Most of us merely survive on what's called the 'little drink' and mind control where most humans don't even know we've taken their blood. Most of us just want to live secluded from society, to go unnoticed in the night and enjoy the simple things in life. But there are those" he said glaring at the Defendant, "Those that believe humans are inferior to vampires and are mere cattle for their claiming. They desire the control their very existence creates over humans and they think they don't have to live by society's rules or laws. They don't try to blend in like the rest of us. They seek superiority, wealth, power, control and use humans as their stepping stones. The Defendant is one of those people. I saw her in action at her party, her obsession with me, and an obsession that eventually lead to her demise."

"Demise you say?"

"Yes. Eventually, all these sorts of vampires are exterminated by either their own kind who grow weary of their antics or by those that make it their life work to hunt vampires. In this case, the very society that she sought control over is the one that is going to be her undoing."

"You are assuming quite a lot there young man."

"No. The Prosecution has the facts, cold, hard, irrefutable facts but if they should somehow fail, the order has already been put out on the Defendants head by the vampire Regime and hunters alike for exposing the vampire race to the humans."

"So, what do you gain by all this, being a vampire yourself?"

"Me? I gain nothing. After this is over, I will fade away into obscurity until the next generation comes around where I will be unknown and can go back to living a normal life."

"Are you romantic with Ms. Fleece?"

"What?" Skendar said caught off guard.

"Are you involved romantically with Ms. Fleece?"

"No. We are roommates, nothing more" he said starting to feel his cheeks flush slightly. Alexis, sitting in the bench was also caught off guard but hadn't considered him again since the night of the sting. She'd had too much else to worry about but now it was brought back to her attention and her cheeks started to flush as well. Mr. Garrison looked from Skendar to Alexis, paused and then sat back down at his table.

"No further questions your Honor." Alexis caught the jury looking between Skendar and herself and started to feel uneasy.

"Court will resume tomorrow at 9pm where the Prosecutor will call their next witness." Mr. Rattler stood up immediately.

"Your Honor, I believe we've called all the witnesses we need to represent our case at this point but reserve the right to call in rebuttal witnesses at a later date."

"Agreed. So the Prosecution will rest and tomorrow the Defense will call their first witness. Thank you jury and I will see you tomorrow evening" she banged her gavel and left the room.

Skendar came off the stand, walked past Alexis and waited for her in the car. She took her time meeting him there for she wasn't sure where to start. She didn't say a word in the car but when they arrived at home, the instant he closed the door behind him, Alexis pushed him up against the wall and attached her lips to his. His reaction was immediate and as passionate as hers as he took her into his arms and ran his hands up and down her body.

"What….are….you….doing?" he panted between her kisses.

"Shut up and take me into the bedroom" she ordered him. He scooped her up and carried her into his makeshift bedroom while she continued to kiss him and unbutton his shirt. He laid her on the bed and she leaned up on her elbows to look at him seductively. He stood there for a moment before stripping down and jumping onto the bed next to her. She shimmied out of her dress and panties and rolled over on her side to continue kissing him which he gladly met with his anxious lips.

Her hands explored his body just as his explored hers. He rolled on top of her and thrust himself inside as she moaned out in pain at his size. Soon, however, she was enjoying it as much as he was. They made love all night long, taking breaks between sessions for drinks and snacks for her. The last time was the most intense. Just as he was on top of her and getting excited, she felt his teeth scrape her neck. Goosebumps ran down the entire length of her body.

"Do it" she purred. He jolted back not realizing what he'd done.

"Do what?"

"Bite me. I want you to" she whispered into his ear. He couldn't believe what he was hearing. Had she really thought about this before now? Maybe he would take a little drink and then they could talk more about the consequences of him turning her when she wasn't as frisky.

With a single thrust, he nicked her neck with his tooth and lapped at the blood that trickled down.

"I didn't say nibble on me, I said bite me" she instructed him and slapped his bare butt. Without further hesitation, he bite full force into the side of her neck as he continued to thrust in and out of her. He knew the euphoria she was feeling from the two combined sensations and knew she'd want it more and more as it was addicting. After he'd drank just enough from her but not enough to turn her, he pulled away and climbed into the bed next to her wiping his mouth with the back of his hand. She lay there on her back, staring up at the sky with a faraway look in her eyes.

"Are you okay?" he asked her.

"Shhhhhh. You're going to ruin the waves of pleasure that are still washing over me" she whispered back. He lay there watching her, not wanting this to be the first way he drank from her. He'd wanted it to be an intimate evening, in front of the fire, just some wine and him tasting her. He knew now however that she would always want it like this for the euphoria that came with sex with a vampire and their bite was irresistible but she couldn't have it. Soon, he wouldn't be able to resist any longer and would turn her. It takes a huge amount of self-control to withdraw for him and he was afraid he'd get caught up in it one night and pass beyond the realm of no return. Another thought came into his mind. 'Did she want him for him or for what he was?' He'd have to read her romantic thoughts, a practice he let go of many centuries ago for he didn't always like having all the answers and the truth sometimes hurt.

However, with her, he'd just have to make that exception which wasn't something he was looking forward to.

She slowly rolled over on her side to face him and he looked into her eyes. They were ones full of passion, ones like he'd never seen from her. She lightly took her nails and ran them up and down his arm and chest. '*She's still in shock*' he thought to himself. He got up from the bed, went into the kitchen and started making her coffee. It was the only remedy to wear off her alcohol induced vampire trance. When it was done, she made her way into the kitchen after him.

"That smells good" she smiled, a little back to normal but he knew she had to drink the coffee first.

"Here. I made it just the way you like it" he said handing a cup to her.

"How do you know how I like my coffee?"

"I watch you make it every day, all day long. You are a coffee junkie."

"Oh. I guess I am" she giggled. She went into the living room, sat down on the couch and started sipping the coffee. '*Good*' he thought. '*The effects should wear off quickly if she continues to drink it.*' She still seemed in a trance of sorts but when she was done with her cup she seemed to snap out of it.

"How do you feel?" he asked hopefully.

"My neck hurts" she said running her fingers across the fresh wound. "Holy shit! What just happened?" she said jumping out of her seat. She was standing in front of the couch with her hands on her hips facing Skendar. He looked at her half sheepishly and half resolutely.

"You told me to bite you" he informed her.

"NO I did not!"

"Yes, I promise you that you did." She stopped and tried hard to remember the situation but it was all a little fuzzy to her. '*The coffee must really be working*' Skendar thought to himself. Alexis flung herself back down onto the couch.

"Am I a vampire now?" she asked with a somber, almost defeated tone in her voice. Skendar came and sat down cautiously next to her. He took her hand in his and turned her to face him.

"No, you are not a vampire. I simply fed from you during sex which gave you a huge sense of euphoria so you kept prodding me to bite harder. I stopped before I would have turned you. I wanted you to be the one during a sober moment to be able to make that decision. We hadn't even discussed it yet so I wasn't sure if it was the euphoria or your true feelings talking. I wanted to give you that option later."

"Thank you" she said, removing her hand from his and placing it in her own lap. "Why don't I remember the sex and this euphoria you said I experienced?"

"I gave you a potion to repress the memory. I didn't want you to make a decision based on your experience. I wanted you to have a clear head to decide if you wanted to be a creature of the night like me." She looked further away from him.

"I don't know if I'll ever be able to make that decision. Your lifestyle is just too hard for me. Just the sleeping schedule alone sucks, no pun intended, and the rest, well…I just don't know about." Skendar's shoulder's drooped. He'd hoped for more from her but how could he be surprised? Who would choose this existence? Suddenly Skendar stood.

"It's almost dawn. I have to go to rest. I'm really sorry about tonight. Please do not think for a moment that I took advantage of you. It was you who attacked me when we entered the apartment. I just followed your lead. Please don't hate me" he begged. She stood, faced him, wrapped her arms around his waist and placed her head on his chest.

"I could never hate you" she said. They stayed like that for a couple minutes before he broke and headed towards his room. She sat down on the couch to think about and try to remember what happened tonight. How much did she care for him? Enough to give him her eternity? Her head started to hurt while attempting to remember so she made her way to her bedroom and fell asleep immediately dreaming about Skendar and her future.

Chapter Twenty: The Defense

The following evening in court, the Defense called Lavina to the stand to get her testimony.

"Please state your name and occupation for the record" Mr. Garrison instructed. She snickered.

"I'm Lavina Miller and I'm a vampire."

"That's your occupation? A vampire?"

"Yes. It's a full time job keeping up with vampire society, feedings, etc. It's very taxing" she giggled but no one else in the court did. She noticed and became somber again.

"So tell us, Ms. Miller, did you have anything against Ms. Fleece?"

"Ms. Fleece you say? I've read about her antics in the newspapers and don't agree with them but have nothing against her personally."

"You mean you didn't know her when she was undercover in the drug cartel sting?"

"Mr. Garrison. There were so many people on the compound. I didn't make it my priority to know every one of them."

"So what about these murders you've been alledged of committing?"

"What about them?"

"Did you commit them?"

"Of course not. I have better things to do than associate myself with human scum. I am an important figure within the vampire community so I have standards and an image to uphold."

"Thank you Ms. Miller. No further questions" Mr. Garrison said and headed back to his table. Lavina started to set down from the witness box when Mr. Rattler spoke up:

"I'M not done with you Ms. Miller. Will you please return to the stand?" She glared at him but reluctantly returned to the stand and sat down with a sickeningly sweet smile. "So, you say you didn't commit those murders. Am I correct in repeating what you said?"

"Yes."

"Then why did you admit to Officer Skendar in the bedroom that you did?"

"I thought he was a fellow vampire and I was lying to keep up my image in the community."

"Lying? Like you are now? Like you are about knowing Ms. Fleece and having something against her?"

"Objection!" Mr. Garrison jumped out of his chair and banged on the table.

"Sustained. Mr. Rattler, watch your tongue or I will place you in contempt of court!"

"Sorry Your Honor" he said lowering his head. "May I continue?"

"Yes but be careful with your line of questioning."

"Ms. Miller, why is it that all the murders you are charged with involve Ms. Fleece somehow?"

"I don't know but I didn't kill them."

"And you say you didn't know Ms. Fleece from the compound yet she was in the room when you were shot. Didn't you recognize her from that?"

"Everything happened so quickly that I honestly can't remember who all was in the room at the time."

"But again, we have you on tape confessing to the murders and your obsession with Ms. Fleece. How do you explain that?"

"The tape was altered."

"Yet a moment ago you admitted to telling Officer Skendar the truth since you believed him to be a fellow vampire and to keep up your image."

"I don't know what to tell you then." Satisfied that he'd placed doubt about her character in the minds of the jury, he said:

"No further questions" and returned to his table.

"Mr. Garrison, please call your next witness. Ms. Miller, you may step down now." Mr. Garrison rose from the table and addressed the Judge.

"Your Honor, the Defense rests at this time." There was a gasp from the entire courtroom. They had expected several character witnesses for the Defense but apparently 'no one was willing to out themselves as a vampire' according to Skendar who whispered such into Alexis' ear. Even the Judge seemed shocked.

"Well then, tomorrow at 9pm sharp we will hear closing arguments and then the case will be handed over to the jury. The jury will now be sequestered for their own safety until a decision has been reached and carried out. Sorry folks but thank you for your service on this case. Court is adjourned." She banged her gavel and left the courtroom shaking her head from side to side still in disbelief.

The ride home tonight between Skendar and Alexis was a talkative one. Alexis couldn't believe the way the Defense operated and didn't really put up much of a fight.

"They don't think she'll be convicted and even if she is, it's very unlikely that they will exact a punishment that would kill a vampire. In the State of Ohio, if a punishment is exacted and the person lives, they are free to go on their way. For example, if they are electrocuted, and live, they are a free person" he explained.

"Really? I never knew that."

"That's what they are counting on. It's much harder to kill a vampire with human's traditional methods. They know this and she's a somewhat strong vampire. She'd survive something like that." Alexis thought about this for the rest of the ride home. That would really suck if she survived her punishment, if found guilty and then go on to put Alexis on the run from her for the rest of her life. "I know what you're thinking. If you were a vampire, you wouldn't have to go on the run from her. Like I said before, there are other vampires and hunters just waiting to kill her should she be released and if you were a vampire, you would be protected under our laws."

"Well, that's something to think about should the occasion arise."

"That's not the only reason to become a vampire though. You really need to think about it before you make your decision. I made my decision out of greed and it's not been a life full of roses. Sometimes it's awful what we have to do and you'd have to be able to live with that for eternity and eternity is a very long time…too long sometimes."

"I know. I have been thinking about it ever since that night. Would you be there with me for eternity?"

"If that's what you wanted."

"But is it what you want?"

"Of course. I've grown very fond of you. You are a very mysterious, strong and loving woman. I would be honored to have you by my side for eternity." She melted in the seat next to him.

When they arrived at home, she attacked him again once in the door and he carried her into the bedroom. They had a repeat of the previous night with lovemaking the entire night and his bite which sent Alexis into a state of euphoria.

"Shall I turn you?" he asked after pulling away from drinking from her neck.

"Not yet but drink as much as you can, it feels amazing" she panted and he went back to tending to her neck. She lay there afterwards in her significant state of euphoria and then fell asleep immediately afterwards. Skendar snuck out of her room into his resting place for the day. He'd been a little disappointed as he thought he was going to turn her tonight after their conversation in the car but apparently she wasn't ready just yet. He would have to be patient.

Chapter Twenty-One: Closing Statements

The next evening, Mr. Rattler addressed the jury with his closing statement. He spoke about how they proved their case with first person testimony and with audio/video evidence. They proved the motive behind the Defendant's killings and vendetta against Ms. Fleece. He went on to explain that he had an unusual method of extermination should she be found guilty to ensure she didn't survive and go free but they had to convict her first to learn what it was. He spoke for almost two hours before turning over the floor to the Defense.

Mr. Garrison claimed that the Prosecution failed to prove anything or any relation between the Defendant and Ms. Fleece. They said they felt confident that the jury would 'do the right thing' and dismiss all charges against the Defendant. He spoke for only thirty minutes before returning to his table. He patted Lavina's knee under the table and she grabbed his hand, twisted it until he quietly gasped out in pain.

The Judge then gave her instructions to the jury. She reminded them that all exhibits presented in court were accessible to them for review again during their decision process. She informed them that they would still be sequestered and that the entire jury must come to the same conclusion. She instructed them to appoint a Foreperson to be in charge of them and to keep their minds on the case and not turn on each other if there's some disagreement. She turned over the case to the jury at exactly 1:30am and instructed them to work on it for the next three hours before retiring to bed. They were to then resume working on the case by 9pm sharp, following this schedule until they reached a decision.

Alexis was on the edge of her seat as the jury filed out. She watched the expressions on each one of the jurors' faces and each one seemed anxious to get started. *'Good. That means it won't take long...I hope'* she thought to herself. Skendar read her thoughts and smiled to himself. She was so naïve but he hoped she was right.

That night Alexis was exhausted and went home and into her bedroom alone. Skendar felt disappointed but realized she had a lot on her mind. He would give her tonight to herself before asking her about it again. She lay down on her bed, fully dressed and fell immediately asleep as exhaustion from the trial and her nights with Skendar finally caught up with her.

Alexis slept until 8pm the following evening and as if an internal alarm clock went off, she jumped up out of bed as if she'd missed something. She checked her phone as Mr. Rattler had promised to call/text when the jury had come back but there was nothing. She stood looking at the phone for a few minutes, clearly disappointed. Should she go out and face Skendar? She didn't know if she was ready for that just yet so she went into her bathroom and drew herself a nice warm bath. She slowly got in as it was extremely warm but after she got all the way in and began to soak, it felt good on her seemly cold body. She'd pulled her hair up on top of her head but strands had started falling down around her face and were wet as well. She must have fell asleep in the tub for she never heard her door open and him sneak into the bathroom.

"You'll prune if you stay in there any longer" came the velvety voice. Alexis' eyes fluttered open and there stood Skendar, holding up a towel in front of his face so as not to see her though she was sure he'd peeked. She stood up and stepped into the towel which he wrapped around her lovingly. He held her there, wrapped in the towel, in his arms and he stared into her eyes. She felt herself giving in to his gaze though she tried to resist. He moved one arm up and pulled the comb out of Alexis' hair to allow it to fall down around her face, framing it like an angel. She gently pushed him a step back, dropped her towel, grabbed his hand and dragged him to her bed where they collapsed into each other's arms.

He tried to pace himself with her by just kissing her and slowly stroking her body. She suddenly took charge and rolled him on top of her while spreading her legs for him. He reluctantly entered her but could smell her blood calling him. The animal in him took over and he began to ravish her body.

"Bite me again" she commanded. He held back and she grabbed the back of his head and pushed his face into her neck. "I said bite me!" He could no longer resist and drove his fangs into the sweet peach that was her neck and began to drink. She tasted better than she had even the nights before. There had been some sort of change in the taste of her blood and he liked it. When they finished sexually, he continued to lay there drinking slowly from her. He took it slow so as to savor every drop. She moaned with pleasure and cradled his head to her neck. Tonight, as he dug his teeth in she saw the sun set and then as he continued to drink she saw an amazing display of fireworks behind her closed eyes. The beautiful lights trailed through the nights' sky as he drank and she felt light headed. When he pulled away, she saw the leftover smoke that floated aimlessly through the night's sky and a smile spread across her face.

"Did you enjoy yourself?" he asked. She smiled even wider. "I'll take that as a 'yes'."

"Of course I did. Every time I'm with you it's like…like…like fireworks" she giggled. "And don't give me any of that coffee tonight. I know your trick. I want to remember tonight for the rest of my life." Skendar gave her a feigned look of shock but fell back into her waiting arms and cuddled with her. "I have to get up early tomorrow and run down to the precinct to talk to my boss. He's only there until 5pm so I'll have to go by myself while you sleep." He looked at her disappointedly.

"You know I don't like it when you go places by yourself" he said trying to scold her. She just laughed.

"I know but Lavina is behind bars and it's not like you can go with me at that time."

"I know, I know but I still don't have to like it." They remained cuddled together in her bed until she fell back asleep. He quietly snuck out of her room after setting her alarm and made a phone call. He called a friend and asked him to keep an eye on Alexis the next day on her outing. After the friend agreed, he made another phone call to Mr. Rattler who told him there was no new information from the jury and they still hadn't made a decision. He hung up satisfied and headed back to bed himself.

Chapter Twenty-Two: Alexis' Future

Alexis woke at 4pm when her alarm went off. Funny. She didn't remember setting the alarm but decided Skendar probably did for her and was grateful. She had to hurry to catch her Lieutenant to see about getting her old job back. She rushed through her 'morning' procedure and flew out the door after grabbing the keys to Skendar's car. As soon as she walked out into the midday sun, her skin started to feel uncomfortable and she felt extremely hot for such a comfortably temperate day. She tried not to pay attention to it, got in the car and cranked the air conditioning. She made her way to the precinct and parked just outside the entrance. The short jog from the car to the building was almost too much for her skin. It was like she'd already been sunburned and the sun was burning it on top of the original burn. She again put it out of her head as she was excited to talk about her job.

She knocked on her Lieutenant's door and he motioned for her to come in though he was on the phone. When he was done, he steepled his fingers in front of his face and just stared at Alexis.

"What do you want me to tell you Alexis?" he asked. She laughed lightheartedly before seeing how serious he was.

"I want you to tell me I have my job back, Sir."

"Well, at this point, I can't do that."

"Why not?"

"With the case still looming over our heads, the higher ups got word about your misconducts…"

"Which I served probation for already" she interrupted him.

"That being said, they're not sure you're still cut out to be a Detective. They think you may be more of a liability than they are willing to take. I'm sorry dear." Alexis couldn't believe she was hearing the words that were coming out of his mouth.

"But I have been on the force five years and have a mostly stellar record" she protested.

"Yes, mostly. That's the key word."

"But if I'm right about this case, doesn't that count for anything?" she tried desperately.

"Unfortunately, your fellow undercovers and Officer Skendar will get the credit for it since you were on probation and needed to be kept out for legal purposes. Surely you understand?" She jumped up and slammed her hand on his desk scattering the papers all over the floor he'd had stacked there.

"Surely I do not! I will take this up with IA and launch an investigation on my own then."

"I don't recommend you do that. They will make sure you won't look favorably and will take away all the department is currently willing to offer you."

"What are they offering?" she sat down still visibly upset, tears in the corners of her eyes.

"They are going to give you severance pay for the next three years and continue your medical coverage for the next five. They will strike your misconduct from your records and give you a transfer of your choosing after that time with a glowing recommendation. It's really a great deal. You should take it Alexis." She thought for a few moments.

"And Officer Skendar?"

"Well, he's being transferred to Detective pending the outcome of the trial" he said sheepishly.

"So he's taking my job?" she bellowed. The Lieutenant got up and closed his door.

"YOU gave him all the power of the take down of Lavina. YOU gave him your job. Like I said, take the package. Take some time off. Decide where you've always wanted to go and then put in for your transfer. It's what's for the best. We'll mail your desk stuff to Skendar's apartment."

"Fine" she said getting up to leave, "But I hope Lavina's killed for your sake or she just may come after you next" she said storming out of the office, slamming the office door behind her.

She stepped back out into the sun to head to her car and couldn't believe how much her skin was burning. It was like nothing she'd ever experienced before and she'd been burned on the beach in Brasil before which was supposedly the hottest sun around. She again cranked the air conditioning in the car and drove back to the apartment as fast as possible.

When she arrived, Skendar was still resting. She closed the door and then wigged out. She threw her purse and keys across the room, ripped off her jacket (literally ripping the sleeve off herself), kicked the corner of the coffee table and flipped it across the room. She stopped, suddenly surprised at her strength, started shaking and sat down on the couch. Suddenly Skendar appeared behind her.

"What happened here? Are you okay?" he asked.

"What's happening to me?" she asked, still trembling. He took her into his arms, placed his chin on the top of her head and read her thoughts.

"Oh dear" he said shocked.

"What's wrong?" she demanded pulling away from him.

"It's happening and it shouldn't be. There's something about you that accelerating the process."

"What process?"

"The change."

"Stop being cryptic. What change, what's accelerating it, what are you talking about?" she demanded, standing up. He grabbed her hand and pulled her down on the couch next to him.

"You are becoming a vampire" he said solemnly.

"What? How is that possible? I never drank your blood and you said you didn't take enough. What did you do? Did you go too far?"

"No! I swear!"

"Then how?"

"I don't know. There's something different about you. I knew it the moment we met but couldn't put my finger on it. There's some gene inside you that is grabbing ahold of the vampire saliva from my teeth when I drink from you and changing you. It's never been heard of."

"Great! Not only do I not have a job, you took my job, Lavina is still alive and I'm an anomaly!"

"What are you talking about?" he asked already knowing the answer from when he read her mind.

"I met with my Lieutenant and he said you got my job, I got severance pay and a transfer of my choice in three years pending a positive outcome from the case."

"I'm so sorry dear" he said taking her hands in his.

"DON'T call me 'dear'! You've done this to me!"

"If I remember correctly, you wanted it, no you demanded it of me ever since you found out I was a vampire. This is as much your fault as it is mine" he fired back. She leaned back on the couch and started crying. Skendar wanted to hold her but was afraid of her reaction. He watched helplessly as she cried, slow, hot tears slid down her face. He eventually handed her a tissue box when she started to sniffle. She snatched it from him, still obviously angry. She got up without a word and went into her bedroom, closing the door behind her, threw herself on her bed and sobbed uncontrollably.

She hadn't decided if she's wanted to be a vampire yet. Even after all her time with Skendar, she still didn't know what she wanted. Now something else was taken from her after she'd lost so much in the past few months between Lavina, her job and now her life. Was she being a little overdramatic? She didn't think so. Her life was about to change, for good and she would have to suck it up and make some decisions. First, she had to find out what 'gene' she had that had accelerated the vampire process. She'd lost her father as a young child and couldn't remember much about him and her mother had been taken by Lavina. Maybe that was the key. Why would Lavina want her mother? She thought it was just to get back at her but maybe there was another reason. Just as she was contemplating that, she heard a knock at the door. The door opened, a hand reached in holding her phone and he said, "It's for you." She jumped up, grabbed the phone and slammed the door shut. She took the phone with nervous hands and sat down on the bed.

"Hello?"

"Ms. Fleece?"

"Yes Mr. Rattler. Is there a decision?" she asked hopefully.

"Yes. It will be given tonight at midnight. I assumed you'd want to be in court."

"Yes, thank you. I will be. Do we have any idea which way the jury is leaning?"

"We have no idea but I have a surprise for them should the circumstances warrant it. That's all I can tell you for now. See you soon." The phone disconnected and she just sat there on the side of her bed holding her phone in a moment of shock. This could be the moment she'd been waiting for and then again, Lavina could go free. What then? Was she ready to deal with that decision yet? If so, it might give her the time she would need with her to find out why she wanted her mother and more about this gene. That was, if Lavina didn't continue to try to kill her.

Chapter Twenty-Three: The Verdict

At precisely midnight, the Judge entered the courtroom just after the jury filed in and took a seat at her bench. Alexis was seated next to Skendar behind the Prosecutor who looked cool as a cucumber.

"Mr. Foreman, has the jury reached its decision?" the Judge asked. An older plump man with glasses rose with a piece of paper in his hand. He handed it to the Bailiff which handed it to the Judge. She read it for what seemed like a very long time to Alexis and then handed it back to the man. "Okay then, to the charges of first degree manslaughter against Ms. Lavina Miller, what say the jury?"

"The jury finds the Defendant...guilty as charged on all counts" the man read from the paper and then sat down. Alexis breathed a sigh of relief yet was she really relieved? Skendar patted her knee quickly and then pulled his hand back like he'd been burned.

"We now move to the sentencing phase of the trial. Mr. Rattler, you said you had a request?" the Judge asked.

"Yes Your Honor. May I address the jury?"

"Objection!" Mr. Garrison declared.

"Overruled! Mr. Rattler, please proceed."

"Thank you. My fellow jurors, thank you for the excellent work you have put into finding the correct verdict for the Defendant. Now, as you've been made aware of, the Defendant is a vampire so conventional means of the death penalty do not apply to her as they won't produce the same end result. So, I propose two options. One, as in olden days, there be an Executioner with an axe who will cut her head off which is a sure way to kill a vampire. The second way is a little less gruesome. I propose we have a dunk tank full of holy water, blessed by a priest on hand and the Defendant is lowered into the water which will consume her entire body and produce the same result an electrocution would provide without the shock of it."

"Objection!" Mr. Garrison protested again.

"Do you have any other options for a death penalty?" the Judge asked. Mr. Garrison fumbled around for a while before finally saying 'no'. "Well then, jurors, you now have to decide one further thing. You need to decide the method of which the Defendant will be put to death. This is usually my decision but since it is such a highly unlikely case, I'd like your opinions. The decision will ultimately be mine but you are still required to take this decision seriously and come to a conclusion. You will now be dismissed and again directed to follow the same schedule as before. Thank you."

"Your Honor? Have you forgotten something?" Mr. Garrison stood at his table smiling.

"What's that Mr. Garrison?" the Judge asked annoyed.

"The Defendant has the right to three appeals." The Judge thought for a moment.

"The Defendant will forfeit her right to the appeal process due to the heinous condition of the crimes that she has committed. Furthermore, it does not behoove the prison to keep her locked up there for the duration of an appeal process so I am revoking that privilege here and now. There will be nothing further" the Judge ordered, banged her gavel and left the room.

The room was immediately buzzing. Mr. Garrison still stood at his table staring at the empty court bench in disbelief at the Judge's appeal decision. Mr. Rattler turned to Alexis, winked at her and shook her hand in congratulations. She tried to put on a brave smile but still had so much turning through her brain that she couldn't fully process what had just happened. Skendar noticed her discombobulation and guided her out to the car and took her home. He could see she was in a state of shock. She kept mumbling to herself, so low that even his vampire hearing couldn't make out what she was saying. He helped her in the house and to the couch. She lay down, he fitted her with pillows and covered her with a blanket before going to make her favorite warm comforting cup of coffee.

Alexis spent the next two night/days curled up on that couch, not reading or talking to anyone. The previous days' events finally had taken their toll on her. Skendar made himself scarce except to wait on her, fluff her pillows, get her tissue and more coffee while she drank almost by the gallon. Eventually, one day, Alexis got up off the couch, went into her room and made an all-important phone call to Mr. Rattler.

Chapter Twenty-Four: The Unusual Request

The following evening, at midnight, court resumed in its usual manner. After everyone was in and sitting the Judge addressed the court.

"Mr. Foreman, has the jury come to a decision on the sentencing phase of this trial?"

"Yes we have" said the man before handing the paper again to the Judge. She looked it over and handed it back. "Go ahead and read your decision." The man cleared his throat.

"It is the decision of this jury, that though her crimes were heinous, a dunk tank of holy water would be a more humane way of extinguishing the life of the Defendant" he said before sitting back down.

"I couldn't agree more" the Judge said when suddenly Mr. Rattler stood and cleared his throat. "Mr. Rattler, is there something you'd like to say?"

"Yes, Your Honor. It has come to the attention of the court the personal vendetta the Defendant had against Ms. Fleece. It is at the request of the victim, Ms. Fleece that she be granted two evenings a week, two hours per evening visitation with the Defendant to get closure before she is executed."

"This is highly unlikely!" Mr. Garrison jumped up shouting.

"Mr. Garrison, this case is highly unlikely. Due to the unjust effects this case and Defendant have had on Ms. Fleece, she will be allowed the aforementioned visitation where the Defendant will be required to answer her questions and provide relevant conversation. That concludes this case. The jury may be dismissed and we thank you for your service" the Judge banged her gavel and left the bench.

Skendar looked questioningly at Alexis who ignored his stares and looked straight ahead stoically. The shock was evident on his face for this was not something he'd expected. Perhaps Alexis thought Lavina held the key to her 'gene' that was affecting her currently. He didn't know but he was sure to find out once she started seeing Lavina for she'd surely confide in him…he hoped.

Chapter Twenty-Five: First Prison Visit

When Alexis arrived and made her way through the prison, Lavina was already sitting in the glass booth. Alexis sat down, put down her notepads and both women picked up their phones.

"Hi" Alexis started.

"Yah. This should be fun."

"Okay, so, I wanted to know about my mother."

"You're mother? I thought you'd want to start with your father first?"

"My father? Why my father?"

"Because I killed him." Alexis' jaw dropped.

"You killed my father?"

"I see your mother never told you."

"My mother knew?"

"Ah, my dear, I see we have a lot to talk about. Good thing we have 30 days until my execution."

"Okay, you wanted to start with my father, so tell me about him. I was young when he died so I have very few memories of him."

"Awww" Lavina said rolling her eyes. "Anyway, your father was a Scientist, working for the regime of vampire hunters. He'd developed many different weapons for the fight. He also had his own side projects that he kept at home away from the regime.

Many were too incredible to believe and others were so secret that he didn't even share them with your mother, The Regime Enchantress."

"The Regime Enchantress?"

"Don't interrupt me. We'll discuss her another time. Back to your father. It was well known that he was working on a potion that would turn a vampire into a human almost completely but he had a hard time finding test subjects. I had started tracking him as his home location was secret to protect his wife but I learned his comings and goings so after approximately five years, I tracked him down while he was defenseless. He was traveling between his home and the office. I ran him off the road and into a ditch. I got to him before he got out of the car and could get to his weapons in the trunk. I slowly tortured him, made him give me his secrets and then drank from him. He was a commoner and his blood tasted as such" she said spitting to the side in disgust.

"That's enough for now. I'll see you later" Alexis said suddenly standing, gathering her stuff and rushing out of the building. She could barely breathe. Was Lavina telling the truth?

How could her father have done such things and her mother never tell her? Was it to protect her? What else was he working on? What was so controversial that it got him killed? Did her mother know about it? Was she connected and that's why Lavina took her? She was still having a hard time breathing.

She drove home in silence, her mind racing. When she arrived at home, Skendar was sitting on the couch on his laptop. He stopped and stood up when she walked in.

"Why do you look so upset? What did that monster tell you?" he asked.

"Too much for me to process right now but I have mad notes to go over."

"You look exhausted. Why don't you let me put you to bed…" She held up her hand.

"I'm sorry. I'm not really in the mood after all that's happened today."

"That's not what I meant, I'm sorry." He hung his head. She walked over, hugged him briefly and then went to her room and drew herself a warm bath to release the tension from the visit. She fell asleep in the tub again but this time woke up because the water was ice cold around her. Skendar had given her the space she needed and maybe she'd been rude to him but she was going through a lot here.

When Alexis hugged Skendar, he'd read her mind and heard the conversation between Lavina and her that day. He felt so bad for her and didn't know how to help. He would get one of his guys to dig into the history of Alexis' father and his projects. Maybe there'd be something interesting there.

Chapter Twenty-Six: Second Prison Visit

Alexis got through security and made her way to the same glass walled booth and it didn't surprise her to see Lavina siting there smiling at her as she walked up.

"Haven't heard enough yet have ya?" she hissed.

"Where is my mother?" Alexis asked.

"I can't tell you that."

"Can't or won't?"

"Okay, won't. My people are working with her to eradicate the damage done to her by your father." Alexis' eyes grew wide.

"He hurt her?"

"In a manner of speaking."

"Tell me more about her. You said she was an Enchantress? What's that?"

"An Enchantress is basically a Witch who, in your mothers case was also a seer, spell caster and more."

"So what did my father do to hurt her?"

"Well, you know your mother was a vampire, right?"

"WHAT?! A VAMPIRE?!"

"I'll take that as a 'no'. Yes, you see, in an event to get to your father, I came to your mother late one night while he was working and since he couldn't protect her I made her a vampire. Reluctantly, this just only fueled your father to work harder against me. He never saw your mother as the enemy and kept her in hiding when the regime insisted she be exterminated. Between the two of them, he with a scientific concoction and she with an herbal, spell binding potion, they came up with the super vampire killer. Only problem was, she was the only one that they'd tried it on."

"What did it do? Obviously she's still alive so it didn't kill her."

"Well, it wasn't designed to 'kill' vampires per se but to modify them."

"Modify them how?"

"Time's up Miss" came the male voice behind Alexis. Had the time gone so fast already? She had so much more to ask. "You must leave now" he tried again. Lavina smiled a sickly sweet smile, hung up the phone and waved 'bye' to Alexis. Lavina knew what she'd done. She'd given Alexis just enough to stew over without giving up too much information. It was going to drive her batty all weekend thinking about what Lavina said until she could come back next week.

When Alexis came home, Skendar was again on his laptop and stood again when Alexis arrived. This time she dropped her bags once inside the door and ran to him for a hug. He read her mind and found out about the days' conversation.

"So sit. Tell me what happened today" he encouraged her. She sat across from him and recounted what Lavina had told her. He listened quietly until she was done.

"Hmmmm. sounds about right."

"What do you mean?" she asked.

"Well, I had a friend of mine check into your father's secret work. He found the same thing but has more details about this potion your mother took. The potion took away the hunger for blood from others for sustenance, allowed them to act more human (being in daylight, able to eat human food-replacing the blood, and much more) but allowed the vampires to keep their vampire powers (super hearing, strength, mind control, living for eternity, etc.). However, by having you, your mother proved that this potion actually created a gene from your father's work where vampires that had babies wouldn't always be born vampires and could be human. They will possess this gene (due to the potion) to be human unless otherwise taken by a vampire. Then they will become the 'modified' vampire Lavina spoke of."

"So, if we hadn't done anything, I would still be completely human even though my mother was a vampire?"

"Exactly! Also, once a human with this gene is mixed with a vampire, they become a 'super vampire' of sorts and will be stronger than the average vampire, despite their age."

"So, I'm like, really powerful?" Alexis joked.

"Yes, powerful but still dangerous to the regime. They've been searching for this combination of scientific, herbal and spell casting potion for years to help control the existence of vampires."

"Yeah. Lavina said her people have my mom and are researching her as we speak."

"Your mom's strong. She went through everything with your father so she'll never give it up to them, especially since they are working for Lavina. I'll start working on finding the laboratory places she's got locally to see if we can check them out for your mom and get her back.

"Would you really? You'd do that for me? I mean, I was never close to my mom but after all I've learned, I'm sure she's kept a closer eye on me than I suspected."

"I'll get working on it. You know I'd do anything for you" he said looking lovingly into her eyes. She looked back up at him and batted her eyelashes.

"Thank you so much" Alexis said before leaning up to kiss him passionately. They slowly undressed their way to her bedroom and climbed into bed together.

"Want to taste MY blood tonight?" Skendar asked. At first Alexis was horrified but then began to wonder what it would taste like. She was already a vampire so what difference would it make? Right? She looked into his eyes and nodded 'yes'. As he rode her from the top, he slit his wrist and placed it over Alexis' mouth. The salty, irony taste of the blood that danced all over her tongue was a little strong at first but then once the euphoria hit her, it was even more intense than when Skendar drank from her. She really loved the feeling. When they parted bodies, she lay next to him, still huffing as if out of breath but it was more about the excitement from the drink. She was officially a vampire now, despite her best efforts before to deny it. She'd loved his blood and understood why vampires craved it so much. She could get used to that part she guessed, something she'd never thought possible.

The following evening, Skendar sat down with Alexis to go over the property tax records his friend found under Lavina Miller.

"The first location, and closest that is registered to her is the office buildings and such at the old Stockyard on W.65th between Clark and Storer Avenues. The property has been abandoned for many, many years but would be an ideal place to hide a vampire and their dealings. If you'd like, we'd have time to check it out tomorrow night, just after sunset."

"Sounds good to me. What time? 10p?"

"Exactly. We can go together with a couple of my friends who hold the latest blueprints of the stockyards. It used to be an actual city type of structure with roads, street signs, mapped buildings, etc. Most people in the 1970's started buying their meat in the grocery stores so the stockyards held on for a while but finally went out of business. The entire property was left standing, stinking and served as a reminder to the residents of Cleveland that their city was in decline."

The next night, the group met across the street, behind the Kmart building with their blueprints and created their entry points and most probable locations. They made their plan and snuck across the street in the shadows. They searched the buildings methodically with finding noting but some animal guts to show for it. The last building they agreed to enter was an actual laboratory similar to a classroom. Here potions were created and experiments were conducted. There were beakers, bunson burners, measuring tubes, labeled potions and much more all over the room. Alexis slowly looked around the room and when she looked up, she saw large cages hanging from the ceiling. They all appeared to be empty except the final one in the back right corner where a leg was seen hanging over the side of the case. Alexis pointed it out and the men lowered the cage to the ground. When Skendar opened the cage and they all peeked in, Alexis was shocked.

"Mom? Is that you?" she asked amazed.

"Lexie dear? Oh my! You must go before Lavina returns!"

"Lavina's locked up in jail."

"That would explain why she's been absent for a while" she said thoughtfully.

"So, Mrs. Fleece, are you able to walk or should one of my men carry you?" Skendar asked.

"Oh. I'm afraid I'm too weak to walk on my own at this time" Alexis's mom said. Immediately, one of the big men scooped her up, threw her over his shoulder and they started their retreat. Once back across the street behind Kmart, the group parted ways and Skendar took Alexis and her mom back to his place.

"There's so much to tell you" Alexis said.

"Oh Lexie, I have tons to tell you too. Things I've kept from you all your life."

"Good. I have some questions for you about my past." Her mom hung her head in embarrassment.

"It's okay, Mrs. Fleece. We've been taking care of Alexis for you" Skendar said.

"Call me Vivian, please." She then suddenly looked from Alexis to Skendar and back to Alexis. She patted Alexis' knee and didn't say another word.

Chapter Twenty-Seven: Third Prison Visit

This time when Alexis arrived at the booth across from Lavina, she was the one with the sickly sweet smile.

"Don't you look like the cat that ate the canary today?" Lavina teased her.

"In fact, I have."

"How's that?"

"It was a little canary, in a cage suspended from the ceiling but it had red hair." The look on Lavina' face was priceless to Alexis.

"Say hello to your mother for me then" Lavina said, almost with no emotion in her voice. "I hope your mother can help you."

"Thanks for your concern Lavina but I'm sure we'll manage. I just wanted to let you know two things today. One, that we are going to be able to do what you have not in duplicating the vampire gene process now that we are paired together. Secondly, this will be my last visit to you. Now that I have so much information from you, that's all I ever really wanted was information. I'd say good luck to you but we all know what your outcome will be. I will see you on October 31st for your execution. Thank you for everything" and with that, Alexis got up and left an opened mouth Lavina just sitting there in shock.

Chapter Twenty-Eight: The Execution

The water tank glass was shipped from the Shu'Tzu Temple in Tibet. The glass was made by the monks there so it was blessed and prayed upon during construction by some form of God/Buddha or whomever. It was brought into the execution chamber and the electric chair was temporarily removed for this procedure. The Priest on duty had bottle after bottle of holy water blessed by the Pope himself in Italy to pour into the tank. The Priest was also to bless the final tank of water after it'd been filled up for surely he couldn't carry enough bottles to fill this huge dunk tank himself. The kitchen staff at the prison worked overnight to smash up garlic with mallets to include into the water. It took all day to assemble the tank and fill it up, then have the water blessing ceremony but by 11pm, everything was ready to go.

Alexis, Skendar and the two attorneys were present in the viewing room. Lavina was brought in wearing ankle and wrist shackles. She was dressed in her 'favorite' dress, a red, formfitting waterfall bottom with mini train and high heels. When Lavina saw Alexis sitting there, she smiled directly at her like she still knew something she hadn't shared but Alexis was beyond caring. Lavina's wrists were tied together with rope and raised above her head. She was raised into the air and moved directly above the tank.

"Ms. Lavina Miller, have you any last words?" the priest asked her.

"Yes. Ms. Fleece, just remember vampires are for eternity, despite your efforts" she grinned.

"Then with that, may God have mercy on your soul" the priest continued.

The mechanism started to slowly lower Lavina into the water. Her toes, then feet and all the way up to her ankles went into the water tank without incident. Alexis looked at Skendar who shook his shoulders back in disbelief. Lavina was then lowered slowly to the bottom of her knees and her body began to convulse and the scent of burning flesh began to fill the room. As she was lowered to her belly button, her body was now convulsing like she was having a full epileptic fit and the skin was burning off below the water level. She let out a blood curdling scream that the participants would never forget. The amount of pain she was in was evident by her tone and the awful sounds that came out of her mouth. You could see pieces of skin floating around in the tank, the pieces that had fallen off her bone while emerged in the water. She was lowered to her shoulders and her breathing became severely labored and she started to huff and puff like she was in the throws of having a thirty-six hour child birthing delivery. The water had splashed up onto her neck as she convulsed and sores opened up and started bleeding into the water. She was then submerged to the chin and she gulped for air. Underwater now was strictly bone. No skin was left on it as it had burned off. She was lowered just to the opening of her nose where she started blowing bubbles through her nose. She began to wiggle around after not being able to gasp for air. She was moved down to her eyeballs which once they touched the water briefly, were burned out of their sockets and fell into the water to float around before shriveling up and dissolving in the water. She was finally completely submerged and you could see the hair fall out of her head. Her ears shriveled up into tiny balls before also dissolving. Finally the skin on her head fell off like a melting wax mask.

She was left in the water for ten more minutes until it was completely obvious that all parts of her except for her bones were gone, according to the medical examiner on hand. She was pulled up from out of the water where just a skeleton hung from the ropes. It was then placed on a waiting gurney where it would be taken later to the crematorium and the bones would be burned.

Before Lavina's bones were taken from the room, the Judge came in and looked everything over. She then made an announcement.

"The bones will be burned but there has been a request for the ashes by an estranged family member whose wish will be granted. Case closed" she said and left the room.

'Estranged family member'? Skendar mouthed to Alexis. She shrugged her shoulders as if to say, 'I don't know'. Who could this be? Was it someone Alexis had to worry about?

Chapter Twenty-Nine: A New Beginning

Alexis and her mom worked very closely in recreating the new potion, keeping meticulous notes and marketing it to the right people. People that would use it in the correct manner. Other vampires that cursed these things about their very existence. It was an underground kind of operation, one where only Alexis, her mother and Skendar knew about and worked at. Skendar was kind of the odd man out but he was their investigator of their buyers so before they sold the potions, Skendar would fully research them and give the okay or the nay. He'd become invaluable to the women's operation and he was just glad to be able to still be close to Alexis who hadn't shown any interest in him again since the end of the trial.

Vivian shared more about Alexis' father to her, including sharing old family photos and many memories which in turn brought the two of them closer together. They were learning how to live as mother and daughter again after all this time. Her mother had returned to the kind, caring and loyal person she once was when it was just she and her husband now that she had Alexis instead of taking her for granted like before the murders and kidnapping. Yet she could see the desire on Skendar's face for her daughter but never questioned her about it for fear of losing her again.

Alexis found her fathers' journal in her mother's storage bin that they cleaned out along with a lot of her father's old things her mother couldn't bear to look at. This gave Alexis some great insight to her father the Scientist and her father her Dad. He'd done everything he could to keep Vivian safe and was even more protective of Alexis when she was born. Her mother told her he'd bought a secret house in the mountains of West

Virginia as their emergency get away plan but she was sure the government took it by now as they hadn't paid taxes on the property in over twenty years.

One night, while sitting alone in her room, pouring over her fathers' journal, she noticed a part of the back inside cover peeling up. She carefully grabbed it and peeled up the entire back cover. Two papers fell out and one was a land deed to a place in West Virginia and the other was a birth certificate but not her birth certificate. It was for a Jaden Miller. Miller? Wasn't that Lavina's name? Did he and Lavina have a child together? What did this birth certificate mean? Was this the person that took Lavina's ashes?

She kept this from her mother for fear of breaking her heart but took it to Skendar for investigation. She sat with him one night as he ran through his online sources and he found that the property was still owned by someone with the last name Miller and the deed had been transferred to them the very year her father had been killed. Skendar had a bad feeling about this but didn't let on to Alexis just how bad he worried about it. He knew how much it was eating her up inside, he didn't need to add to it. He simply put an arm around her shoulder and to his surprise she leaned into his chest and placed her head there. She was exhausted, he could see it in her mind. There'd been so much for her to process since the end of the trial and this was just one more thing.

"I'll take care of it" he whispered to her. She simply nodded into his chest just before starting to sob. He leaned down and kissed the top of her head. He wouldn't let anything happen to her. He'd waited this long for her, he could wait until she was ready.

The following evening, Skendar was in his room packing when Alexis entered and dropped her light backpack on the foot of his bed.

"What's this?" he asked having a bad feeling he already knew the answer.

"I'm going with you."

"Where?"

"To West Virginia."

"Oh no you're not. I told you I'll take care of this."

"But if I have a half sibling, I deserve the right to know him don't I?"

"What if all he wants to do is kill you? What if he wants retribution for being shut away for over twenty years? What if he wants vengeance for the death of his mother, the only family he had left?"

"I realize all that but I still have to know. I have to see for myself. Does he look like me? Is he a vampire? There's so much I want to know."

"What if he won't give you those answers?"

"I have to at least try or I'll always wonder 'what if', ya know?" He let out a growl, knowing he'd lost the battle and she was going no matter what he said. He packed even lighter, grabbed her bag and the two of them snuck out of the house.

"What'd you tell Vivian on where you'd be?"

"I told her I needed some time away with you" Alexis smiled sheepishly.

"And she fell for it?" he asked, not surprised.

"Hook, line and sinker."

The two of them traveled the 300 miles from Cleveland to Bethany Pike, West Virginia. It was in the pan handle of the state, between West Liberty and Follansbee Townships, up on the side of the mountain with a large creek that ran on the other side of the road. There were no street lights and they were lucky the roads were even paved. They followed the mile markers until they came upon the parcel number listed on the deed. Sure enough, there sat on the side of the mountain, a small little house, probably only two bedrooms and very old fashioned.

As they approached the house, they noticed there were no lights on in the house.

"See, no one's home. Let's go" Skendar said, half-jokingly.

"I didn't come this far just to see the outside of the house. Let's sneak in and take a look around."

"Do you really think that's a good idea?"

"Of course not but it's what we came for."

They went around to the back of the house and the back door was unlocked. They quietly made their way inside, thankful for vampire night vision which Alexis had also developed. They moved through the kitchen and the moment they stepped into the living room, with Skendar leading of course, a light next to the window chair flicked on.

There sat a young man, about Alexis' age, with her eyes, nose and mouth structure. He could almost have been her twin. The resemblance shocked both of them yet neither breathed a word at first.

"Did you really think you could sneak up on me?" came the voice of the man sitting in the chair. "I could smell you the moment you got into Wheeling." He looked around Skendar to talk to Alexis, "I knew you'd come." She jumped back, startled.

"Me? Why? How do you know me?"

"I saw you in the courtroom every day of my mother's trial. I saw you testify. I saw you visit her and I saw you rescue your mother I LET you rescue your mother. It's hard to be without a parent" he said suddenly sad.

"So, you're my brother?" Alexis asked, voice shaking.

"Half-brother, yes." Skendar took a step closer to him.

"I wouldn't do that if I were you" he said raising an axe that had been sitting across his lap. "I mean neither of you harm but I will defend myself."

"I'm sorry for him, he's just protective" Alexis said stepping in front of Skendar and he motioned for her to sit on the couch across from him. Skendar stood behind her at the ready just in case.

"If you knew about me, why didn't you contact me?" Alexis asked Jaden.

"I didn't want to disrupt your life more than my mother already had. I had no idea about your past involvement with her as a Detective, I only knew what she told me about you in regards to my father."

"What did she tell you about him?"

"That he was a good man and loved his wife very much but she wanted his potion. So when he wouldn't give it to her, she turned his wife, your mother into a vampire. She wanted a child and begged him to bed her but he refused. The night she ran him off the road, she seduced him, right there in the woods, had him sign over this place to her, tortured him for his secret vampire potion and then killed him when he refused." Alexis cringed when he said 'tortured'. "I'm sorry but you asked" he said delicately.

"It's okay. So, you were there in the old Stockyards? Waiting for the breakthrough with my mother for the potion?"

"Yes. My mother didn't want me to have to live as this monster for the rest of my life. She thought mating with a human would make the offspring a human also but it did not and here I am. I have limited existence, I don't go out except to feed and that's usually off animals as the population around here is sparse. I hate what I am and she knew how much I hated it. She hated to see me miserable and she blamed you in a way. Your mother was a vampire when she got pregnant with you but thanks to the potion, you came out human."

"I'm not human anymore" Alexis said sadly.

"I know but that's because of him" he nodded towards Skendar. "Now, with the potion, you will be one of the most powerful vampires alive. You will have the best of both worlds, human and vampire."

"Not all vampires want to be human" Skendar finally spoke up.

"No, but I do." Alexis' heart started to break for Jaden. She rummaged through her bag and brought out a little green vial.

"No! You can't!" Skendar tried to grab it away from Alexis. She looked at him with sad eyes.

"I have to" she said to Skendar. He knew he couldn't stop her so he backed away even though he disagreed.

"Here" Alexis said handing the vial to Jaden.

"What's this? Poison?" he asked.

"No. It's the potion. Take it and stop being alone. You can be human again and have a human child with a human wife and no one will ever have to know you are half vampire ever again." He looked from the vial, to her and back to the vial again before slowly taking it.

"Thank you" he whispered.

"You're welcome" she said and with that, she and Skendar left the house, never to return.

Chapter Thirty: Revenge

The ride home was dead silence between Skendar and Alexis. Each one disagreed with what had just transpired but knew discussing it now would only cause an argument so they kept their thoughts to themselves. The ride home seemed much longer than the ride there did to both of them.

When they arrived home, Vivian was still asleep so Alexis and Skendar went their separate ways into their own bedrooms, still without a word to the other. They both tossed and turned in their fitful sleep, neither one willing to go to the other. On the ride home, Alexis realized how powerful she now really had become. She would have all the abilities of the vampire yet be able to blend into society with humans. How cool would that be?

The next morning, Vivian was awake just after dawn and went downstairs into the basement to start working on a new batch of potions. Several hours into her work, she heard footsteps coming down the basement stairs. She was surprised that Alexis and Skendar would be back so soon but what she saw amazed her even more. There, standing at the bottom of the stairs, stood a young man with Alexis' eyes, nose and mouth structure. His skin was more of an olive skin but his features strikingly resembled her daughters. Fear suddenly filled her insides.

"Do you know who I am?" asked the young man.

"No dear. I'm sorry. Should I?"

"Yes. I am your husband and Lavina Miller's son." Vivian collapsed to the floor in disbelief.

"I...I...I didn't know..."

"You didn't know your husband had an affair? You mean your daughter didn't tell you?"

"My…daughter?" she said gasping for air.

"Yes. She came to see me last night and gave me some of your potion. Now I am like her, thanks to you. You were at the Stockyards to cure me but your mangy daughter rescued you before you could cure me. Then, bless her tender heart, she came knocking on my door and just gave me the potion. That's some girl you've got there."

"She's a great girl. You leave her alone" Vivian said, trying to stand up and swing at him but his mind control over her made her weak and her heart slow making her too dizzy to stand.

"Don't you worry about her. Once I'm finished with her, I'll be back for you and together with your potion and my contacts we will rule the world!" he laughed. "Now where is she?"

"She's away…with her boyfriend."

"We'll see about that" he said and started back up the stairs to search the house. When he found her resting in her bed, he thought, 'this is too easy'. He quickly placed duct tape across her mouth and bound her wrists and ankles. She awoke suddenly in a panic just as he was lifting her over his shoulder and carried her out of the house into the trunk of the waiting car. He took her to his house in West Virginia, chained her to the bedpost in his mothers' old bedroom, locked her in there and waited. It wasn't her he was really after. It was Skendar. Alexis was just an end to his means. He knew by taking Alexis, Skendar would come blind with a vengeance after him and he could exact his revenge against him at that time. The last time he visited with Alexis was not the time. He needed Alexis' sympathy and that potion he was counting on her bringing. He was now stronger than Skendar thanks to the potion so he was prepared.

The moment Skendar opened his bedroom door, Vivian was standing there in a panic.

"He took her!" she bellowed and crimpled into a ball on the floor sobbing.

"Who took who?" he asking trying to remain calm.

"Lavina Miller's son took my daughter!" Skendar's skin suddenly turned hot. "He came in here, told me who he was and took Alexis while you slept!" she said accusingly. He ran past her and outside where his man was waiting at the door.

"Devin followed them to the house in West Virginia. He's waiting for your directions" said the man.

"Drive. I'll call him on the way" Skendar instructed. When he arrived, Devin was waiting down the road for him. He instructed the men to find Alexis, break in and rescue her while he dealt with Jaden but to be undetectable in the process.

Skendar cautiously walked up onto the porch and brashly walked through the front door. Jaden was sitting in the same chair by the window waiting for him.

"Where is she?!" Skendar demanded.

"She's fine. I'd be more worried about your own skin."

"I'm not worried about me. I'll be fine."

"I wouldn't be so confident."

"What do you want little man?"

"You wronged my mother and I'm going to finish her dying wish."

"What was that?"

"To kill you."

"Why would she want me dead?"

"You don't remember? Ha ha!" he mocked Skendar who was starting to lose his calm and getting irritated. "Please tell me you remember your Maker?"

"Of course I do" Skendar said irritated.

"Your Maker was also my mother's Maker. He had promised you to her when he left her but you never came. You were supposed to come take care of her and give her the baby she so craved yet you never showed up. What happened to you?"

"I don't have to answer to you."

"Yes you do!" Jaden shouted at the brink of insanity.

"I'd had a dream, the night I was turned, of a red headed beauty, a human beauty that would come my way if I were patient. There was no way I was going to give up on that dream for the promise from a Maker that left me alone to fend for myself only to reappear centuries later with demands."

"My mother was crushed and alone for many years when you denied her. That is another reason she wanted rid of Alexis because she had what my mother wanted, you."

"I'm really sorry for how your mother suffered but you cannot promise a person to another person. People are not property, even coming from a Maker and your mother was a fool to believe him from the beginning."

"A FOOL?!" he shouted. He lunged at Skendar with his silver crucifix blade aimed at his heart. Skendar easily parried Jaden who went crashing headfirst into the end table, breaking the lamp that had been sitting on it. At the same time of the crash, Skendar's men broke into the window to Alexis' bedroom to extract her but not before she heard everything that had transpired between the two men in the living room. They handed her out the window to each other and rushed her to the black suv to wait for Skendar.

He picked up Jaden and threw him across the room again who crash landed into the lit fireplace. The young vampire's anger was getting the better of him and he couldn't see straight. He got up quickly, brushing off the hot embers and charged at Skendar again swinging the blade at him wildly. Skendar had taken the fire poker and as Jaden was in midair, Skendar drove the poker through Jaden's heart who then fell to the floor dead. Skendar then went out back and grabbed the axe that was stuck in a block of wood and brought it back into the house. He cut off the head of Jaden and then threw both pieces into the fireplace and watched them burn. He returned to the suv and instructed Devin to stay and make sure the entire body burned to ashes and then they were to be scattered into the creek in front of the house.

When Skendar entered the suv, Alexis threw her arms around him and hugged him tightly. She'd been so scared, not just for herself but for him as well. She'd realized, while chained up and waiting for him, just how much he meant to her. He'd been there through everything she'd endured since that night Rodriguez tried to kill her. He'd been so kind and though he'd lead to her turning into a vampire, she'd had the potion and would beg him to take it in the future too, something she was sure he didn't want to do.

On the ride home she leaned into him and asked,

"Who are the two men who rescued me?"

"Ever since the night you arrived at my house, I hired them to watch you. There's actually two more so there was around the clock surveillance on you. I knew you were special and wanted you protected at all times."

"Though I resented you, I knew you were special too" she said and leaned over and kissed him passionately. "I never knew you'd dreamed about me but I'm glad you did."

"Me too" he said, falling back into her arms and pressed his lips to hers.

Chapter Thirty-One: Resolution

When the couple arrived back home, Vivian was waiting at the door to greet her daughter.

"Mom? What are you doing up past your bedtime?"

"I couldn't sleep not knowing about you and seeing that you were alright for myself."

"Thanks mom" she said and hugged her mom.

The two women went into the living room, sat down on the couch and did some catching up. Alexis and Vivian decided to stop making the potion even though there was high demand for it and they could have made a mint. They decided that some things were better left to the universe and didn't need their interference. Vivian moved to a small house down the street and Alexis and Skendar kept the house they'd been staying in.

Alexis and Skendar grew very close again. They'd become intimate now that she'd put aside some of her anxiety and could enjoy what she had around her. They decided to travel the world together in their newfound love for each other. They never married as the next century they'd have to do it all over again and that would be a hassle. Plus, it was only a piece of paper and it was what was truly in their hearts that mattered. Skendar had finally become the King he'd always wanted to be and finally had his Queen by his side for all of eternity. He knew the Regime would come for them eventually. He just hoped he could protect her from them.

36240476R00082

Made in the USA
Middletown, DE
27 October 2016